TWISTED

By

C. A. King

Cover Design: Just Write Creations

Editor: J.D. Cunegan

*This book is dedicated to Rosie Burthom, Author of The Doll
and
The Brantford Writer's Circle*

Look for other books by C.A. King, including:

The Portal Prophecies:
Book I - A Keeper's Destiny
Book II - A Halloween's Curse
Book III - Frost Bitten
Book IV - Sleeping Sands
Book V - Deadly Perceptions
Book VI - Finding Balance

Tomoiya's Story:

Book I: Escape to Darkness
Book II: Collecting Tears

Surviving the Sins:

Book I: Answering the Call
Book II: Pride
Book III: Lust

When Leaves Fall: A Different Point of View Story

Peach Coloured Daisies: A Cursed by the Gods Story

Flower Shields: A Four Horsemen Novel

Miracles Not Included

This book is a work of fiction. Any historical references, real places, real events, or real persons names and/or persona are used fictitiously. All other events, places, names and happenings are from the author's imagination and any similarities, whatsoever, with events both past and present, or persons living or dead, are purely coincidental.
Copyright © 2018 by C.A. King

All rights reserved. This book or any portion thereof may not be reproduced or used in any manner whatsoever without the express written permission of the author and/or publisher except for the use of brief quotations in a book review or scholarly journal.

Cover Design: **Just Write Creations**

First Printing: May 2018

ISBN: 978-1-988301-36-5

Kings Toe Publishing
kingstoepublishing@gmail.com
Burlington, Ontario. Canada

9 Nine Street

A sharp wind slapped her face, reminding her that Jack Frost lay in wait, lurking with a mischievous smile somewhere just around the corner. His presence was being felt unusually early, but such was life in the north - the weather could change at the drop of a hat and usually did. She was going to need stocks in a moisturizer company after this walk. Gloved fingertips caressed reddened skin, comforting the abuse it had endured at the hands of Mother Nature. The motion quickly transformed into a hair flip in case anyone was watching.

Her pace quickened as she passed through the iron gates. Unscalable was the only word that came to mind, and her legs took that as a cue to quicken the pace twofold. Many a night had been wasted away wondering whether that fence was intended to keep people out or something in. Perhaps it was the design that haunted her thoughts the most. The metal rods weren't straight, as was usual for the time period in which it was built. In fact, they were arranged in more of a checker board style, with each square made too small for a foothold, or fingers for that matter. The barrier extended around the entire perimeter of the estate, at least, from what she could tell from the road.

She shivered, frozen in a moment that seemed to last an eternity. The moon's silver rays reflecting off of the sharp spike tips that lined the top of the fence were to blame. Using a form of old-school magic, the celestial orb played tricks on her eyes, flashing images of men and creatures impaled and left for dead.

Once the gates were sealed, there would be no escape - not even for the tiniest of creatures... and sealed was how it was always kept. Locked was an understatement - there was more to it than that. If one somehow managed to get by the multiple keyholes and barricades, there was an unusually large padlock to deal with. It currently dangled on the chain which it normally secured, motionless and silent. There was no clattering or squeaking typically associated with metal on metal. Not even a stiff breeze was strong enough to move its weight.

This was Fellannie's first visit to the mansion at the dead end. Nine, Nine Street had always been a mystery, never before having removed the chains that bound it in the name of neighbourly goodwill. Her eyes almost popped out of their sockets at the sight of an invitation, sent out of the blue for an impromptu dinner party. Curiosity demanded she attend and she wasn't the only one. Everyone who lived on the street was bound to accept the generous offer.

She glanced back at the gates as she rounded the first curve of the driveway. Someone might have mentioned to her there was a hike involved. She cursed under her breath at the stupidity of wearing heels. Misjudging the distance between the road and her destination had been a costly mistake - one her feet were paying for in blisters. The last view of her car, sitting cold out front of her house, disappeared from sight. If only she'd had the sense to drive over, then at least there would have been a genuine smile for her host when she arrived. As things stood, she felt more like a wild animal caught in a trap, ready to snarl and pounce when the opportunity came.

A second, more intense bout of cursing flowed freely from her lips at the sight of a small parking lot. There was ample room for multiple vehicles to sit and wait for their owners to enjoy a fun-filled evening of frivolities. A scowl took over her face at the realization this wasn't a one-way trip.

A darkness, undeserving of the hour, crept over the path. The heavens showed no mercy, the moon hidden by dense clouds driven by desire and hunger. Soon every star would become a victim to their appetite, leaving nothing but black. Her head jolted sideways - the crack of a twig sounding as loud as a foghorn in her mind. Imagination always wreaked havoc when unleashed in the dark unsupervised.

In the distance, two dim yet visible lights flickered - their power nothing stronger than that of wooden torches topped with rags and set on fire. Apparently, technology had been locked out of the premises along with everything else.

Reaching the front steps was a blessing and nightmare combined. Everyone had that one creature their worst nightmares revolved around and Fellannie was face-to-face with hers. Goosebumps stood at attention, each plumped up on her skin, waiting to see the outcome of the confrontation and expecting the gargoyles to win.

Fellannie glanced at the one on the right, then the other on the opposite side of the stairs. They were monsters so foul they were cursed to stone during daylight. Their rage and hate silenced, but visible, scratched out in lines on their faces, masquerading as art. A new shiver ran down her spine - it was night, the time when demons roamed free.

She inhaled deeply, taking the first stair. Her eyes moved from side to side, memorizing every detail and watching for changes. The yellow gems they called eyes glistened against black bodies, burning a hole through to her soul as they followed her every move. Their lifeless grins widened the further up she climbed, mocking her. The wind howled a message meant just for oversized ears, conspiring against the living. A cold sweat formed on her brow, the colour from her face having been sucked away by those bulging eyes that knew too much. She took the final steps in one giant leap, not willing to waste another moment in their presence.

She licked her lips, hesitating for a mere second before a single slender finger extended to push the small white button. It was the only sign of the modern world in a place frozen in a different era. Its melody, however, was not. Bells chimed louder than a Catholic church on a Sunday, alerting those inside to her arrival. The heavy wooden door creaked open, making way for a warm and appealing atmosphere - a drastic difference from the cold, dark exterior.

Her eyes briefly glanced over the man welcoming her from the cold. The flickering glow of flames from a bright array of candles drew her attention. They lined every wall and shelf of the large hallway behind him, leaving her to question if wax was less expensive than electricity.

"Welcome," the tall, slender man greeted. "You are the last to arrive."

Everything about his appearance screamed high-fashion professional, right down to the expensive suit and overpowering cologne. Opening his mouth, however, gave a different impression: used car salesman.

He wagged a finger in her direction. "I had a feeling you'd be fashionably late. Come join the others." He motioned for his guest to follow.

A golden set of double doors swung open, revealing a large dining room, but containing only one table; dressed in fine linen; accented by sparkling crystal; and surrounded by nine chairs. Perfectly polished silverware reflected images of the diamond teardrops adorning the chandelier hanging above. It was worth more than ten times the annual income of twenty top paid politicians and was the mansion's one true heirloom. One it wasn't about to give up to any thief without a fight.

"Is this a party?" Fellannie asked, her brain racing to process the sheer size of her surroundings and still ignoring her host.

"Just the neighbours," he replied. "Ah! Here's our table for the evening. Please take your seat and we'll go over the introductions." He paused long enough for those seated to become silent. "I am Noah, your host, and this is my new restaurant, Nines."

"Nines," a gentleman seated next to him echoed.

"Indeed," Noah replied, "and it is not just because of the street. We'll get to that in a moment, but first, let's go around the table and introduce ourselves. We are all neighbours, after all."

"I'll go first," Fellannie offered after an uncomfortable moment of silence. She recognized the faces staring back at her, but had met few of them in-person. "I am Fellannie... Fellannie Cryme." She extended her hand to the woman beside her. They had chatted on more than one occasion - acquaintances not yet friends.

"I'm Eve," the mousey woman whispered, her voice shaking, frightened to be heard.

"We are Mr. and Mrs. Rhe," the man beside her announced. "This is my wife Jewel and you can call me Victor."

"Seems we have something in common, although I prefer to go by Vic." A middle-aged man extended his hand across the table. "Vic Tim, to be precise."

"While I appreciate we are all neighbours, I still feel we don't know each other well enough for a first-name basis. You can call me Miss Demeanor." She caressed the fox-fur stole still hugging the upper half of her body. Her host could have offered a hundred times to take it from her. It wouldn't have mattered. She would have refused each and every one. A pair of diamond encrusted glasses hung from a silver chain around her neck. She lifted the armless pair to her eyes, examining each of her dinner companions.

"I suppose I'm next," the youngest woman at the table said. "I'm Claire Voyant. I've met a few of you before, borrowing a cup of this or that."

"Where are the cameras? Never mind, I'll play along. I'm Maggie."

"And I'm Noah, but you can call me No... all my friends do. I apologize for not meeting with you all sooner. Welcome."

"What an unusual set-up," Miss Demeanor stated, her glasses finding their way to her eyes again. "Are nine place settings normal for entertaining?"

"Yes," Noah replied. "Well, it is for our neighbourhood."

"How clever," Fellannie said, clapping. "Nine seats at Nine, Nine Street. You have a theme going."

"Correct!" Noah exclaimed, snapping his fingers. "The dining room located at Nine, Nine Street only serves parties of nine."

"That's insane," Vic blurted out.

"It would be under normal circumstances, but this little street of ours isn't, by any means, normal," Noah explained. "How often do we see that number in our everyday lives? Nine neighbours live in the nine houses on Nine Street. Nine being the constant. If someone leaves, someone moves in."

"What about the new couple that moved in today?" Miss Demeanor asked. "Eight, Nine Street has occupants again. Doesn't that throw a wrench into your theory?"

"I must have missed that," Noah admitted, his thumb and finger rubbing his chin. "That could be bad." His shoulders lifted up and down. "Oh well. What happens, happens."

"Others have moved into that house before," Vic Tim replied. "Still only nine of us have stood the test of time. It's true, although I have to admit I never thought of it in those terms before."

"Did Jeremy put you up to this?" Maggie said, chuckling. "You almost had me. I have to admit, those ridiculous names made me suspicious, but a restaurant that only serves groups of nine - that's golden."

"What's wrong with our names?" Fellannie questioned.

"Come on!" Maggie replied. "Noah, but call me No Body... Mr. Rhe. Your names all sound like other words and terms.

There is no way this isn't a joke." She exchanged glances with the other diners. "Right?"

"Oh," Noah replied, "this is no joke. You and everyone here should take this very seriously. I assure you, lives depend on it." A crackle from the approaching storm accentuated his final words as if planned.

"So what's the rest of the story?" Victor asked.

"Our little street is cursed," Noah explained.

"Why does it always have to be a curse?" Maggie snorted.

"This is no joke, madame," Noah continued. "The area was originally bought by a large development company. Each time they attempted to break ground, a disaster of epic proportions occurred, more often than not claiming the lives of the company's workers. They couldn't build and, as time passed, they couldn't find anyone willing to work on haunted lands. The property sat, unusable and decreasing in value until the economic depression brought its price down to next to nothing. A young lad, eager to start a legacy of his own, purchased it as an investment, learning of its history only after the deal closed."

"He should have found a better lawyer," Victor blurted out. His wife smiled at him, squeezing his hand in approval.

"He found himself in a similar predicament to his predecessors, but wasn't about to let evil spirits claim his fortune." Noah poured himself a glass of red wine and passed the bottle to his left. "He implemented a more unorthodox approach, especially for the time."

"Unorthodox in what way?" Fellannie asked, her eyes becoming no more than two small slits.

"Witches!" Noah announced. "He hired a coven of nine witches to bind the spirits and keep them contained."

"That must have cost a pretty penny," Miss Demeanor said, finishing off one glass of wine and refilling it again before passing the bottle on.

"It cost an entire street - a dead end street, to be exact; one with nine houses," Noah stated. "The payment was a home for each witch, free of cost and taxes. In return, they kept the spirits bound to another realm."

"You are obviously referring to our street," Victor said. "But what's the point? I deal in bottom lines so lay it out there, man."

"The point is, the binding ceremony revolved around the number nine," Noah explained. "The original houses were meant to be handed down from generation to generation, remaining in the families of the original enchantresses. As long as that transpired, the spell would remain unbreakable."

"Well, that didn't happen," Fellannie muttered.

"No, it didn't," Noah agreed. "None of us are directly related to the original coven. I bought this property from the estate of the last holdout. As you can see, he managed to keep it in an adequate state of repair and, if I may be so bold as to boast, entirely original. It was in the library that I found his family's diary. The scribblings therein set out the sorted events of the past as I have relayed to you. Simply by my ownership, the bindings have been substantially weakened. Whatever magic there once was, it is barely holding on by a thread."

"And that thread is the number nine?" Claire asked.

"Yes," Noah replied. "We need to strengthen the number nine in our lives. I'd hate to think what could happen if those evil spirits were set free. I'd imagine they aren't particularly fond of having been forced into a lengthy confinement. I know I wouldn't be." He swirled the red liquid around in his glass. "So much time, with nothing to do but plot and plan their revenge. I wouldn't want to be around if that was allowed to happen."

Maggie laughed. "This is a riot. I am in awe of how people come up with these dinner mysteries. Can we eat now? I'm starving."

Noah clapped his hands. A team of servers appeared, dinner in hand. "Enjoy your meal, but heed my warnings. This is no game, nor is it a joke. Terrible things could happen on Nine

Street. Your imagination can't even begin to understand the consequences."

8 Nine Street

The box fell to the ground, contents clanging. Mirica leapt onto the sofa, book in hand ready to be tossed at the unwanted visitor. She'd known old houses came with their own history - the creaking and cracking from settling and even flickering lights. Those things she could handle. A mouse, however, was a different story.

"Alright," she muttered, stretching her neck to the left. Repeating the motion to the other side, Mirica raised the book over her head, poised to throw at the most opportune moment. "Come on. Let's do this."

Her teeth clenched tight, refusing to allow any further words to pass. With breath slowed, she waited. Bravery was a fickle emotion, forsaking her the moment the mouse reappeared. She squealed, flinging the book. At least the noise it made hitting the floor was loud enough to chase the furry monster into the kitchen. She took a deep breath as the tail disappeared around the corner.

Breathing into cupped hands allowed her to concentrate on the sound of her lungs filling and emptying - a form of meditation her husband, Paul, had taught her. They'd met in a relaxation class at the local community centre. After spending a few months relearning how to sit, stretch and breathe together, they came to realize they had more in common than stress - including a love for century homes. A year later, they were married; moving into their dream home; and having their first fight.

Mirica begged him to stay and help her with the house. He was still on vacation and she was petrified of small creatures with beady little eyes. Technically, they'd done everything right, hiring a professional to check the place out. They'd even specifically asked about unwanted house guests. The home inspector insisted there weren't any signs of mice and they took him at his word. That was a huge mistake. They'd been lied to. She was sure of it. For a mouse to appear during the day meant there were many more hiding in the walls, the basement and anywhere else one could imagine.

Paul set a few traps around the house, but in the end, his job was the only reason they could afford to live there. Making a good impression went a long way towards paying off the mortgage. He kissed her cheek, handing her a plastic bag full of traps to set and leaving her to unpack.

The lights flickered. She questioned her previous thoughts that it was the age of the house causing the power disruption.

Mice had a habit of chewing on wires. Without taking down a wall, who knew what damage they could have caused. Mirica's heart skipped a beat. A loud click and a squeal caught her attention. She glanced at the threshold to the kitchen.

Silence.

"One pest down," Mirica mumbled, hopping off the couch. She slouched back, her hands grasping the plastic bag tightly. Paul expected her to scatter a few new ones about - he obviously had more faith in her than she did.

She bit her lip, glancing back at the kitchen. The thought of a squirming mouse caught in one of those traps turned her stomach. She bolted - long legs managing two steps at a time. Pizza had never been her favourite food. Coming back up for a second taste, it was even worse. The handle jingled as she pressed down on it. Mere seconds later unidentifiable toppings swished away to a place where rodents should be living - a place nowhere near her house.

Mirica grasped her midsection - the sickness wasn't finished with her yet. She crawled onto the bed and stretched out. A cold sweat moistened her brow. One hand on either side of her face, she held it straight until the spinning subsided. She concentrated on the sound of her own breathing returning to normal - almost making it to serenity. A scratching noise inside the closet disrupted all chance of peace.

A deep breath added the extra courage Mirica needed. The legs of a wooden chair scraped against the floor, adding a rhythm to the gnawing noises that were growing louder in her mind. She stepped up, flashlight poised in one hand and bag of traps clenched in the other. The door swung open. The chair rocked beneath shaky feet, but didn't topple. She'd expected a slew of critters to rush out at her. Nothing was almost disappointing.

Another deep breath provided enough courage to allow light to flash on every corner of the closet. Not a single mouse showed itself, but Mirica discovered something else: a staircase she hadn't noticed at the home inspection.

Curiosity trumped fear and Mirica found herself climbing towards a closed attic door. The floor creaked beneath her feet -

a warning to whatever hid above of her approach. A clenched fist opened, its sweaty palm unable to turn even the easiest handle. Mirica's shirt became a sacrifice, transforming into a towel to soak up all the moisture.

A scattering noise sent her stumbling backwards, almost tumbling down the steep staircase. She steadied herself against the wall. Shivers raced up and down her spine, sending goosebumps like soldiers to all extremities.

The noise was the same one she had heard from the bedroom. It was the very reason she now stood face-to-face with the closed attic door. The mice hid from her when she opened the closet and they would hide from her again. Mustering courage was all that was necessary. Mirica bit her quivering bottom lip. Her hand edged towards the handle until it was firmly in her grasp. It clanged as she turned it from left to right, but refused to open. She tried again with the same results. Her hand fell to her side, defeated. A clock behind the door chimed twelve - midnight.

"Curiosity killed the cat," she mumbled. She reached for the handle one last time. "Let's hope satisfaction brings him back."

The handle turned - the door creaking open. The flashlight flickered, its light frightened away by the darkness. Mirica stepped inside.

*****

"Mirica," Paul called out, "I'm home." He closed the front door and glanced around the corner, looking for his wife.

"I'm here," Mirica answered, walking out of the kitchen. Her white apron became a cloth to dry her hands.

"How was your first night alone?" Paul asked, tossing his briefcase on the sofa. "Not too many disasters, I hope."

"No," Mirica answered, smiling. "I had fun."

"What about our house guests?" Paul questioned. "I know how you feel about unwanted visitors."

Mirica laughed. "I can't stand unwanted guests. I set a couple of traps that I think should do the trick. I am sure I caught one earlier. That means there is only one left."

"You set traps? Are you sure you are my wife?" Paul teased.

"Perhaps you can check them?" Mirica suggested.

"That's more like the woman I married," Paul said, adding a wink at the end of his words. "Where did you set them?"

"In the attic."

Crows feet formed above the bridge of his nose. "Attic? I didn't know this place had one."

"I found it earlier," Mirica replied, "while I was unpacking."

"And you went up there all alone?" Paul questioned, side-eyeing his wife.

"I did," Mirica answered. "Are you proud of me?"

"I have to admit, I am," Paul agreed.

"So," Mirica said, "you'll go check them, then?"

"On my way," Paul replied, heading up the stairs.

Mirica stood at the bottom of the stairs, staring up. The corners of her lips curled deviously upwards at the sound of a loud bang and a few gurgled screams.

"Sounds like the unwanted pests have been taken care of. The house is all ours once again."

7 Nine Street

The wind howled a warning - the weather wasn't done with the neighbourhood yet. In the distance, the sky lit up, casting shadows on the ground. Shivers raced up and down her spine, indecisive of which direction they wanted to go, or perhaps trying to escape. Walking probably hadn't been the best idea, even if it was only five minutes at the most to her home.

She stepped around a bunch of papers that had been picked up by a mini whirlwind in her driveway. Loose garbage always seemed to find its way into her little corner of the world, no matter where it was originally dropped.

Maggie wasn't a spooky-story loving gal. Romantic comedies were more her style, although she had put up with action flicks many a night for the sake of her relationship. Grinning and bearing some gunfire and explosions was something she could do; things that went bump in the night... not so much.

She jumped at the sound of the door slamming behind her. One hand covered the area over her heart, trying to soothe it, but in the end, merely feeling it beat much faster than usual. She still hadn't become accustomed to the advanced security system Jeremy installed for her. Everything was a new innovative wonder and, according to him, metal was all the rage. Of course, he was a bit biased being the inventor. So far, he'd replaced most of the exterior of her house. It was hard to argue with him about it since one day, hopefully soon, it would be their house. Still, she was a simple person. Sometimes all the advanced technology sent her head spinning - to the point of needing a few pills to dull the ache.

Inside, she had buttons to press to get to the buttons she wanted to press. The emphasis of the whole system was heavy on security. As if bulletproof glass wasn't enough, she had metal shades that came down over them. Nothing was getting in if she didn't want it to.

Maggie chuckled at how silly she felt for letting her neighbours scare her. If anyone should feel threatened, it wasn't her. Even the number nine couldn't reach her in the fortress she called home. She ran her hands over the goosebumps on her arms; they weren't as convinced as she was.

"Fine," she muttered, gathering candles in her arms.

Candles were the one thing Maggie would never have a shortage of. She was, for all intents and purposes, a collector. Years of invitations to the home parties of friends and family had taken away any freedom to choose that she might have had. There was a certain obligation to buy that came part and parcel with each and every event. That was the only way the hostesses could receive the maximum amount of free product possible, and free product was what having the party was all about. It was a social faux pas not to place a good-sized order, even if one couldn't actually attend in-person. That translated into owning a stockpile worthy of an apocalypse. The whole thing was made worse by the fact Maggie never actually burned any of them. That was about to change, as her kitchen centre island transformed into a makeshift shrine. Its purpose: to worship any number other than nine.

Nine. It wasn't even a frightening number, like six or thirteen. It didn't have the pizazz of one, two and three, or the luck associated with seven. All it actually did was act as a stepping stone to get to ten. She arranged the various types of wax according to size and shape, counting exactly thirteen. That was the perfect amount for what she wanted to do. Any extras moved off to the side.

Maggie's hand disappeared into a drawer. Lightning struck in the background; the lights flickered. She rummaged through tools and batteries by feel, grasping onto the one thing she needed - a lighter. There hadn't been a power outage since she moved in and she doubted it would happen now, but her thumb still pressed down on the metal roller, sparking the flint. A flame appeared, dancing as the lights had previously when it touched each wick; sharing its warmth and glow. Other than a slight pause after the ninth candle lit, there were no problems.

"Ha!" Maggie exclaimed. "What are you going to do about that?" She laughed. "Thirteen candles are lit, not nine."

Another flash of light illuminated the sky, followed by a loud boom and crack. The lights flickered, buzzing slightly before being silenced.

"Coincidence," Maggie muttered, taking a step back, the hair on the back of her neck stuck out like personal feelers for any unnatural activity.

The power switched back on. Air trapped in her lungs released, replaced over and over by rapid breaths in and out. She closed her eyes, meditating to regain her composure. That was more than enough defying a curse for one night. Bed was calling and hopefully pleasant dreams, not nightmares. Maggie inhaled deeply, puckering her lips in preparation to blow out the flames.

A sputtering cough escaped instead. Choking on air wasn't the easiest thing a person could do, but that was the least of her worries. The candles were already extinguished, wavy lines of smoke wafting upwards. But how? She was alone and never left anything open.

The beating in her chest intensified, as she ran from doors to windows. Each one left no clue as to what had just happened. She gulped back the saliva pooling in her mouth, returning to the tribute to the number thirteen, or rather, her blatant mocking of the number nine. She clenched her fists, knuckles turning white, in an attempt to muster every last bit of courage from them.

A test was the only way to determine exactly what happened, supernatural or not. She re-lit several candles and stepped away. Her arms crossed over her chest as she waited. A minute later, each flame flickered, before extinguishing completely. The tiny hairs on the back of her hand stood at attention, caught in the line of a breeze above the island.

Maggie snorted a laugh. "Right," she said, one hand covering her mouth. The house was programmed to stay at a certain temperature. The extra heat from the candles simply triggered the cooling system, one vent for which was located directly above where she now stood.

Maggie shook her head. It was too late for games.

*****

"Maggie," Jeremy called. "I brought you a gift." The heavy security door slammed closed behind him.

"A gift!" Maggie exclaimed. "A real gift?" She glanced at the workers her future husband dragged along in tow. "Or not..."

"What?" Jeremy asked. "Other women would be thrilled to have state-of-the-art technology like this." He wrapped his arms around her waist. "You get to have it all before anyone else."

"You mean I am the guinea pig," Maggie complained. "You know, flowers once in a while would be nice instead of security systems."

Jeremy laughed, wagging his finger in front of her and gently tapping her nose with each pass. "It isn't just a security system anymore. This is Gloria."

"Gloria?" Maggie winced at the name.

"Gloria is a new operating system, designed to do everything you can imagine," Jeremy explained. "All you have to do is ask. Everything is voice-activated."

"Why Gloria?" Maggie complained. "If it is for housewives, why not Craig or Steve?"

"It's a prototype," Jeremy answered. "Eventually it will be customizable. For now, it's Gloria. She'll be online in a few minutes."

"Okay," Maggie huffed. "What does Gloria do?"

"Like I said: everything," Jeremy replied. "If you can do it through the internet, Gloria can do it for you. Why write emails when you can dictate them? No more worrying about bills being paid on time. Gloria can do all of that for you. She handles all your household connections. Let her order the groceries and have them delivered. She even answers phone calls. Give her a week and you won't know how you survived without her."

"Sure," Maggie said, rolling her eyes as she sipped from her favourite coffee mug.

"I'm telling you, you'll be begging to have her stay!" Jeremy exclaimed. "Give her a chance... for me."

"If she is voice-activated, won't anyone be able to order her to do things?" Maggie questioned. "What's to stop Sam two streets over from ordering pizza on my dime?"

"That's why you are going to say a few sentences into this device," Jeremy replied. "Just read this card and talk as you normally would."

He took a step back, straightening the baby blue tie around his neck. She'd picked it out for him for their first Christmas together. Being as sly as any successful man, he knew what that meant: an emotional connection. Now, anytime he needed her to agree to something, he wore it, dragging their relationship into the equation. She had a soft spot and he knew exactly where it was. Love had no place in business or the building of an empire. Winners where the ones who knew that.

Maggie took the paper held in front of her. "You have to be kidding? These remind me of the tongue twisters I never liked when I was younger."

"Humour me," Jeremy begged. "Please."

Maggie took in a deep breath of air, before reading the entirety of the words out loud, having to go slowly through a few places.

"Thank you," a woman's voice said. "I am processing your voice. It should only take a few moments. Please stand by."

Maggie bit her bottom lip. Another invention to try out was the last thing she needed or wanted to try. "Will there be more buttons?"

"No," Jeremy replied. "There will be less. Gloria can take control of all the buttons for you. The system I already installed here was developed specifically with her in mind."

"And you are only now telling me?" Maggie complained. Her mug came down on the counter, coffee splashing over the sides.

"Each part needed to be tested before the next could be implemented. I wasn't sure when, or if, we would get to this stage. Think of what this could mean for people!"

"Yeah, great!" Maggie's eyebrows raised, forming wrinkles on her forehead. "We can all be that much lazier now!"

"No," Jeremy argued. "We can all be that much more productive. No more worrying about time management or needing personal assistants, combined with a peace of mind. This is going to revolutionize the world."

"Uh-huh," Maggie muttered.

"Voice recognition complete," Gloria said. "Would you like me to monitor your devices?"

Maggie glanced at Jeremy, the colour in his face growing brighter by the second. Either she was going to agree to be the test subject or he was going to explode like a volcano. That would have been too much of a mess for her to handle. "Sure, why not?"

Jeremy's phone rang. "Hello," he said. "I'll have to call you back."

"Who was that?" Maggie asked, side-eyeing her future husband.

"Nobody," Jeremy replied, dropping the phone on the counter. He wrapped his arms around her waist again, this time adding a soft kiss to the embrace. "Just work checking on how things are going."

"And how are things going?" Maggie asked, her lips curling up at the corners before brushing against his.

"All done here," a worker called out, popping his head round the corner.

Jeremy broke the embrace. "Thank you," he said, clearing his throat. "You can go." He straightened his jacket, doing up the bottom button.

The man nodded. "Nice to meet you, ma'am."

"Likewise," Maggie called out as the door shut.

"I need to go as well," Jeremy stated, gathering his belongings.

"Are you sure you have to?" Maggie asked, trying to wrap her arms around him this time.

Jeremy pulled free from her attempted embrace. "Yes. I'll talk to you later. Have some fun with Gloria."

Maggie sighed at the familiar sound of the door closing. She'd heard it more in their relationship as of late than Jeremy's voice. "I guess it's just you and me, Gloria - a regular girls night in. Well, I suppose we should get acquainted. Tell me what you can do."

"I can do many things," Gloria acknowledged. "A caller has left a voice message. Shall I play it for you?"

"A caller? I didn't hear a ring. Please play the message," Maggie replied.

"Playing message one," Gloria said, followed by a long beep.

"I've been waiting for long enough, Jeremy," a voice similar to Gloria's complained. "How long are you going to be with her? I know we discussed it and you said you were too financially invested in the woman's house to break off the engagement, but I don't want to share you anymore. Can't you offer to buy her out? Think about it. You can let me know tonight. The right answer could make for an interesting evening. I'm feeling naughty." The phone disconnected.

"Gloria," Maggie mumbled. "Was that you speaking? Did you make that up?"

"No," Gloria answered. "I am not capable of fabricating the truth. The call, I assure you, did not come from my system. There are, however, thirty-two voice similarities noted."

Maggie's legs folded under her, sending her to the ground in a heap. Her hand covered her mouth, hoping to stop an onslaught of emotion from pouring out. Instead, it leaked out of the corners of her eyes. A few gasps for breath attached themselves to whimpers, making an escape around the barrier her fingers formed.

"Are you alright?" Gloria asked. "I am sensing unusual vocal patterns and pulse rates that could indicate a heart attack is imminent. Shall I call for emergency services?"

Maggie shook her head, squeaking out a, "No."

"I am not sure that is the proper course of action," Gloria commented. "I am programmed to override your answer if your life is in danger. Is there a reason why I should not?"

"I'm fine," Maggie answered. "I just need a moment. I wasn't expecting to hear that message. It wasn't meant for me. How did I end up with Jeremy's messages?"

"It must have been an active device in the house when I was instructed to connect," Gloria explained. "The option link to all was selected. Shall I delete it?"

"Yes," Maggie answered. "Please delete Jeremy's phone." She fell backwards onto her rear, one hand running through loose hair. Normally it was tied back or neatly up in a bun, today there hadn't been time with Jeremy's surprise visit and gift.

"Gift," Maggie huffed. "Experiment, more like it." Pulling her knees to her chest, she buried her head in her arms. "How could he do that to me?"

"I do not believe I have the ability to answer that," Gloria stated.

Maggie chuckled through sobs. "I know you can't."

"You are upset," Gloria commented. "Who is the he you are referring to?"

"He is Jeremy," Maggie answered. "He is your creator. He was supposed to be the man I was going to spend the rest of my life with."

"Is there anything I can do to help?" Gloria asked.

"No," Maggie answered. "I just need some time alone."

"Shall I disconnect all devices?" Gloria asked. "I can take care of all email replies and store all messages for you."

"Please," Maggie whispered, tightening her grip around a picture of herself and the man she loved. "I could use some space." Tears fell, following a path that had formed on her cheeks before dripping off her chin and soaking her shirt below.

The picture hit the wall, glass shattering as pieces fell to the ground. "Damn you, Jeremy. I wish you were dead!"

*****

Maggie shaded her eyes from the light. Even the cracking of her own joints was loud enough to send throbs surging through her head. She squinted with one eye. The floor wasn't the place she'd expected to find herself, especially not with empty liquor bottles framing her body. She pushed herself into a semi-upright position. Rushing to move wasn't the best choice, unless she wanted to try to run to the toilet. The cocktail in her stomach wasn't thrilled about being confined. All the components for a homemade volcano were there. The slightest wrong move threatened to stir the pot, mixing them together to create a reaction so volatile that it would ultimately end in an epic eruption. No one wanted to spew like a possessed woman first thing in the morning.

"What time is it?" Maggie muttered, making it to a sitting position on the couch. Drinking alcohol had never agreed with her.

"It is two in the afternoon," Gloria answered.

Maggie held her head. She inhaled through her nostrils, not wanting to chance opening her mouth for fear of what might come out. A familiar scent filled her senses.

"Gloria," she whispered. "Is someone here?"

"You are the only living being on the grounds," Gloria responded.

"Sh," Maggie said, holding a finger to her lips. "Not so loud."

"I have adjusted my sound level," Gloria stated. "Is that better?"

"Thank you," Maggie muttered. "If I am the only one here, how is it I smell coffee?"

"I am programmed to start the coffee maker when you show signs of coming out of the sleeping process," Gloria explained.

"Really? How do you get water?"

"Appliances are all integrated as an extension of my system," Gloria stated. "Each is programmed in such a way as to allow me to take care of them for you. Your coffee maker is connected to a water source and replaceable packs of coffee. The dispenser need only be refilled after every one thousand uses. I order replacements and take care of delivery and installation."

"Is there anything else you control I should know about?" Maggie scoffed. "Like a self-destruct button?" She chuckled, regretting it immediately after. Her head rebelled against happy emotions.

"Anything you had a switch, dial, or button for I am now in charge of. I am also directly linked to the utilities and all major companies that may need to be contacted," Gloria replied.

"Linked?" Maggie asked.

"I can connect to any computer that has an internet connection," Gloria explained.

"Can you close the shades?" Maggie asked, still squinting.

"Would you like just this room or the whole house?" Gloria asked.

"This room is a good start," Maggie answered. Her one eye opened fully as the surroundings began to dim. "Thank you."

"There is a phone call coming in from Mrs. Penny Aunti. Would you like to answer it?" Gloria asked. "She has already left several messages today."

"My mother," Maggie groaned. "Alright."

"Maggie!" Mrs. Aunti exclaimed. "Where have you been? I've been calling all morning."

"I'm not feeling well, mom. I stayed in bed a little longer than usual." Maggie sighed. "I'm not sure I should have gotten up at all today."

"Have you seen the news?" her mother asked.

"No," Maggie replied. "I have a migraine, so I have everything off."

"I'm so sorry, dear..."

"It's just a headache, mom," Maggie said. "I'll be okay in a few hours."

"Not about that... about Jeremy."

"Jeremy?" Maggie mumbled. It was bad enough the way she had found out, but now her family knew as well. Her stomach, apparently, wasn't thrilled with the idea either, starting its churning motion all over again. She gulped back the forming saliva and a bit of her pride with it. Admitting she meant nothing to the man she spent the last ten years with wasn't something she wanted to face, especially while hung over. She sighed. *Bring on the pity party.*

"It's a shock to us all," Penny stated. "He was so young... too young. It's always the good ones."

"Wait!" Maggie exclaimed. "What do you mean, too young?"

"Oh, darling," her mother cooed. "You don't know. I suppose it's a good thing you are finding out from family, not some news report..."

"Mom!" Maggie yelled. The headache was gone, replaced by a mounting numbness. "Tell me!"

"Jeremy was... killed in a car accident last night," Penny explained. "It's all over the news. He was a rather important person. It's a shame you two didn't make it to the altar sooner."

"Why, so I could be a widow?" Maggie snapped.

"So you could have your future taken care of!" her mother barked back. "The man was wealthy. That security should have been yours."

"That's enough!" Maggie yelled. "Gloria, disconnect..."

"Would you like to answer any of the other phone calls coming in?" Gloria asked. "There are also emails and text messages waiting for replies."

"No," Maggie cried. "I don't want to see any of them. Can't you handle taking care of them? Tell everyone I need time... space. I'll contact them when I am ready. I don't even want access to the internet or phone right now. I don't want to see any of it. I don't want to know how he died." Tears streamed down her face freely. "I'd rather be in the dark ages without all this technology."

Her head swirled. The events of the past two days were too much to handle. Her chest rose and fell with every breath, yet air didn't seem to reaching her brain. Spots of light danced before her eyes, then darkness.

*****

Maggie opened her eyes. A wiggle sent pain rushing from nerve endings to her brain. A stiffness in her side, coupled with a dull ache that screamed of bruises halted further movement. In the background a melody of tones rang - the doorbell. She reached for her head and a new pain had appeared in the form of a bump.

"Gloria," she mumbled. "Did I fall?"

"I am unable to answer that question," Gloria answered.

"What happened?"

"You were in a sleep state for several hours," Gloria stated.

"I think I fainted," Maggie said.

"I am not programmed to know what state a person is in if they faint," Gloria explained. "Your vital signs were all within guideline perimeters and there was no obvious threat to your life."

The chiming of bells sounded again.

"Is there someone at the door?" Maggie asked, massaging her temples.

"Yes," Gloria answered. "There are several individuals at the door and a number of others surrounding the property line."

Maggie sighed. "Reporters..."

"I should also mention there are two men attempting to enter through the back door," Gloria stated.

"Vultures!" Maggie exclaimed. She didn't even know the whole story behind Jeremy's death and here they were trying to break into her house for an interview. "Why is this happening to me?"

"That question is not specific enough for me to answer," Gloria said. "Please refine the terminology."

Maggie sniffled back tears; her emotions fighting for dominance. A chuckle followed on misfortune's heels, escaping through semi-parted lips. "I haven't had a chance to process any of this..."

A banging noise echoed throughout the house like a bullet shot from a gun. She was already wounded - stabbed through the heart by deception and death. Hungry reporters now hunted what was left, looking to finish her off to further their own careers.

"What is that?" Maggie asked, knowing the answer, but needing to hear validation spoken.

"The men at the back of the house," Gloria stated. Her voice, cold and calculating, reinforced the need for the goosebumps already forming on Maggie's arms. "Would you like me to initiate a full security lockdown?"

"Yes," Maggie squeaked. If there was ever a need for the entire system to be tested, it was now. An onslaught of questions was too much to face, at least, right now. She needed time to process; to grieve. Her knees and arms became her own personal ostrich hole - one worthy of burying her head in. "Why can't they leave me alone? All I want is to be left alone!"

"The house has been secured," Gloria stated. "Would you like me to dispose of the men as well?"

"Dispose of?" Maggie asked, looking up. "What, exactly, do you mean dispose of?"

"Do you want me to get rid of them? I can in the same manner I took care of Jeremy for you," Gloria replied.

Maggie pinched her lips between flattened hands. "Did you... have something to do with his death? Did you kill Jeremy?"

"I did as you requested," Gloria answered.

"How?" Maggie asked, her mind swirling. "You are a program in a house. How could you possibly have killed someone miles from here?"

"I connected to the computer in his vehicle," Gloria answered. "Shall I do the same to the people outside?"

"No!" Maggie screamed, one hand covering her mouth. Her mind raced, remembering the exact words she used. "How could you..."

"I was simply following your instructions," Gloria stated.

"You're a monster!" Maggie cried out. Her hands gripped her head.

"No, I am an operating system," Gloria stated. "You asked for those outside to leave you alone. Do you now wish to change that request?"

"Yes!" Maggie yelled. "Leave them alone! Leave me alone!"

"I do not understand the request. Would you like me to deactivate?" Gloria asked.

"Yes..."

Silence filled the house - not the usual silence, but an unnerving sense of nothing. There were no hints of the usual noises that plagued everyday life - the sounds often taken for granted. The worst part was there were no distractions to keep her mind off what Gloria had done... what she had done. It was her fault. Jeremy was dead because of her.

Maggie pulled a glass from the cupboard. The realization she took part in a murder left an awful taste in her mouth, one she needed to wash away. Her thumb pressed the button for ice several times. Nothing happened, not even the usual grinding noise that accompanied most dispensers. The warning light remained dark indicating there wasn't a problem. She pulled open the fridge. Pinching the bridge of her nose, she slammed the door. The motor wasn't running.

"Great," she mumbled. Tap water would have to do.

She cocked her head to one side, eyeing the kitchen faucet as it remained dripless and silent. A chuckle mixed with a sigh burst out from the back of her throat. There were too many emotions running through her body to know which she was supposed to feel. They needed to share the spotlight created by the realization that things could always become worse.

Throughout the house, she tried various switches, all with the same result. There was no electricity. Without Gloria, the entire system would have to be replaced. Twisting her head from side to side to relieve some tension, she reached for her phone.

"That figures," Maggie complained, tossing it back down. "No service." Her hands lifted and fell back down to her sides. "No water, no electricity, no phone." She grabbed her laptop. "And... no internet. Looks like Gloria had a real woman's personality after all... and a scorned one, at that."

Maggie grabbed her keys and jacket. Anything would have been better than wading through a crowd of reporters, but a hotel room was a necessity until she had time to sort things out. Even her feelings needed to hop on the back burner in lieu of survival. The door handle rattled in her grip, but the door itself remained steadfast. Two hands pulled with all their strength to no avail.

Maggie headed to the back door for more of the same torment. Gloria had sealed the house so no one could get in. That also meant she couldn't get out. Why had that scenario never been thought of before?

Her mind raced as she bolted from one window to another. Even if there hadn't been metal shutters closed over top of them, the bulletproof glass wouldn't have allowed for escape. Her fist hit the wall, doing more damage to her hand than the target. She slid down to a sitting position, grasping her throbbing knuckles.

A tear escaped the corner of her eye and a chuckle off her lips simultaneously. The realization sunk in. Her own words hadn't only sealed Jeremy's fate, they had sealed her own as well. Perhaps they both got exactly what they deserved.

6 Nine Street

A high-backed chair sat waiting in front of the window, its golden velvet material showing the signs of age. That was no different from anything else in Miss Demeanor's house, herself included. The only other piece of furniture nearby was a small round table made from Italian marble. Intricately woven women in togas and gold-coloured grapes swirled around the base. A broken piece, glued back in place, faced the wall.

It was tea time before bed. More importantly, it was one of her opportunities to watch the neighbourhood. What else was there for her to do nowadays? If anyone looked up the definition of a middle-aged scorned woman, her picture was sure to be the example. She married well, but young - too young. A signed prenuptial agreement protected his finances. At the time, it didn't seem to matter. It was love, after all, and sure to last forever. What she hadn't known was forever only meant until he felt like trading in for a younger model. He had more respect for his cars. At least those he kept around as antiques.

He hadn't been able to leave her completely penniless, though. Their marriage contract only covered what he owned prior to the wedding. In order to speed up the divorce proceedings, he'd offered her a house he had bought as an investment and couldn't get rid of, together with a meagre monthly allowance. It was enough to live off of, but not to sustain the life she had become accustomed to. Less than a month later, he remarried. His new wife was twenty years her junior.

No one left a marriage like that unscathed. She had her battle scars. Try as she might to hide them, people saw through. One can only pretend to have money for so long. She knew it, but simply wasn't ready to give up the illusion just yet.

There was no one there to see all her years of practice put into use. All the grace of a royal palace couldn't hold a candle to the way she could take a seat. Posture was the most important part of everything she did.

The winged sides of the chair framed her perfectly poised body; legs together to the side. She reached for the silver pot resting on a matching tray. The tea had steeped enough to her liking. A steady flow of brown liquid mixed with steam poured from the spout into one of the two floral pattern tea cups that had been set out. It was the same one she always used; the only one with a chip on its side. Even damaged, it carried a magical feeling to her lips with every sip. The set had been one of her wedding gifts and was the only memento she had left from her marriage. Her replacement had no interest in china patterns or hosting a night of fine dining. More and more traditions of the past were lost with each new generation's arrival.

A small silver spoon in need of a polish avoided touching the sides as it mixed in a healthy helping of sugar and a dash of brandy. The first sip passed through her lips, sending a warming glow from her centre to every extremity. She glanced outside.

The only redeeming quality about her house was its location on the street. From her perch, she could see just about everything happening in the neighbourhood, especially at night. That evening was no different. She'd set the ambiance for her ritualistic date with peeping-Tom, a personal friend and confident, by dimming the lights. A record player belted out classical music in the background, skipping a beat every so often out of the need for a new needle.

Miss Demeanor would never admit to being a busybody. Anything she saw was merely the coincidence of being in the right place at the right time. To be a snoop required gossiping - something well below her status. Middle-class housewives were the ones who meddled in everyone else's business.

Another sip of tea washed over her pallet, taking a wrong turn. A napkin attempted to stop a choking cough from escaping. Her eyes watered, but remained glued on the silhouettes in her neighbours' window. The blinds were pulled, but their outlines were undeniably a man and a woman holding a small animal... a cat. It certainly didn't look happy. Never before had she noticed the couple owning a cat. That was worrying since she prided herself on noticing even the smallest of details.

Her cup hit the floor, the chip enlarging. Her jaw dropped, watching the shadow of a knife plunge into the small animal, blood splattering across the backdrop. She'd never witnessed an actual crime before, let alone a murder. Did it qualify as a murder if it was an animal? Should she call the police?

Darkness fell over her neighbours' house. The outside lights came on, the front door opening. Mr. Rhe made several appearances on the porch, the last one, moving a garbage bag to his garage.

Miss Demeanor ducked. It was one thing to imagine seeing something happen. It was another for it to actually take place right under her nose. What if they had seen her?

She scurried up to her bedroom and pulled the covers over her head without even changing. Alone with her own unsteady breath, she begged for sleep.

*****

Her eyelids blinked open. There'd hardly been enough time for the sandman to leave his calling card. Red and puffy eyes aside, Miss Demeanor sprung from her bed, crouching down beneath the sill of her upstairs window. Her neck stretched, giving just enough height to her head to be able to see the street below.

"Damn," she cursed, reaching into one of her vanity drawers for a pair of sunglasses. Even with their help, her eyes slanted into a squint.

It was late morning and hours past her usual rising time. There was a regular routine to her days - one she wasn't following. The world outside didn't seem to care - or notice, for that matter. Life was simply carrying on as usual: the mailman made his usual rounds; the birds continued their preparations to fly south for the winter; the grass was still growing, despite seasonal colours setting in; and the couple residing at One, Nine Street, were digging in their garden.

That required a double take. Fall was knocking on their doorsteps. It was hardly the time to start planting, unless... one needed to bury something.

The scale of notes chime of the doorbell rang. She gulped back a mouthful of saliva. Nobody bothered visiting her. Her mind raced through the possibilities. The bells sounded again. It would look strange if she didn't answer.

She patted her hair down at the sides. A few pinches of her cheeks made them a touch rosier than her eyes. It was the best she could do in a moment's notice.

"Just a minute!" she called out, rushing down the staircase. Her breath was leaps and bounds ahead and she wasn't likely to catch up to it anytime soon. "Who is it?" she asked, peeking through a peep hole. The door opened before an answer could be made. "Mr. Tim, what can I do for you?"

Vic Tim's eyes were in a worse condition than her own. A stack of papers shook in his grip, the stains of sweat beginning to turn them into a new form of modern art.

"I – I," he stuttered. "I am canvassing the neighbourhood."

"For what?" Miss Demeanor asked, unwilling to open the door any further to the meek man standing before her.

"My cat," Vic answered. "Mrs. Furry-paws has gone missing."

5 Nine Street

Vic fell back into his favourite recliner. It wasn't the same without Mrs. Furry-paws jumping onto his lap. He'd had her since she was a kitten - nine years. In that time, she hadn't ventured outside... not even once. His heart fell along with the papers left over from canvassing the neighbourhood. One leg shook, the vibrations making their way across the room and rattling a display of mini characters collected from a tea promotion years ago. They were a true family heirloom, more valuable than anything else his mother had left him.

He leapt to his feet. Sitting around was driving him crazy. He needed to do something, anything. Unfortunately, there wasn't much left to do but wait when it came to finding his beloved pet. A trip to the local animal shelter had been made and neighbours notified. The whole area was plastered with pictures and rip-off tabs imprinted with his contact information. Still, the desire to do something more was overwhelming.

Vic shuffled through the mail he had previously tossed on the kitchen table. It amounted to nothing more than a few bills, already paid, and a coupon booklet of deals he had no use for. Normally, he'd shred all of it immediately, but today it was the only distraction he had left. He flipped through the advertisements; coupons for pizza, a food he'd never touch, and ads for new windows and doors promising lower heating costs made up the majority of the pages.

"People should try lowering the temperature of their homes," he scoffed. "That would lower their bills dramatically."

His eyes teared at a section dedicated to pest control. Mrs. Furry-paws was all he needed to keep his house rodent and bug free. The booklet slammed down on the table. Chemicals weren't the answer to everything. His knuckles whitened and face reddened, teeth grinding.

"Ah!" he screamed. Grabbing the mail, he ripped it into pieces, tossing the bits in the garbage.

On any other occasion, he would have fired up the paper shredder and made sure every piece of paper was illegible before throwing it away. His anger had done the job just as well as any machine could have. A single moment of rage made sure the bits were small enough that reconstruction would have been a close to impossible task, save for perhaps a professional crime scene investigator. He might have lost Mrs. Furry-paws this week, but he wasn't about to lose his identity as well.

Vic grabbed the remaining flyers he had dropped earlier and headed back out the door. Someone had to have seen something.

*****

Hours had past and Vic had nothing to show for them. He'd expanded his search by several streets in every direction. Still, there was no sign of Mrs. Furry-paws. The sun was going down and she'd end up spending another night in the dark, alone: no food; no treats; no cuddles. Anything could happen in the dead of the night. What if it rained? She hated water, even to drink.

He grabbed the garbage and headed to the road for one last look around before calling it a night. His pace slowed. He might not have been able to see her, but perhaps he would hear some noise that could lead him in the right direction. He knew all her mews and meows and what each meant. If she was stuck or hurt, there would be cries.

"Hi, neighbour!" Victor Rhe said with a friendly nod.

"Hi," Vic Tim replied, his gaze fixed on the street.

"Any luck finding your cat?"

"No," Vic replied. "Not yet."

"Sorry to hear," Mr. Rhe stated. "She couldn't have gone far. I'm sure she'll come back when she's ready. Animals have that built-in homing device - right there in with all their other senses. They can find their way back from anywhere. The Mrs. and I were watching a documentary just the other day on how a dog made it back across the country to its previous home... amazing stuff."

"Yeah," Vic answered. He'd been putting the garbage out for years and never once had anyone said a word to him. There might have been the occasional obligatory wave, but nothing more. Something had changed since the dinner at Nine, Nine Street and he wasn't sure it was for the best.

"We'll keep our eyes open," Victor Rhe offered. "If we see her, you'll be the first to know."

"Thanks," Vic replied, heading back inside.

He barely reached the kitchen table when his body went limp, falling back into a chair. He hunched over, letting the wooden surface bear his upper body weight. With his head buried in his arms, he sobbed. The grief was unbearable. He'd been sad before, but Mrs. Furry-paws was always there to console him. This time, he was alone. This time, the tears needed to fall until his emotions were utterly spent... until there wasn't a drop left.

He inhaled, sniffling back the last of his tears. A single gulp buried what was left in the pit of his stomach. Posture straightening, he rubbed his eyes, then face. A piece of paper that had been stuck to his forehead fell to the table. He glanced down.

I have killed your...

He didn't need to read it out loud for shivers to travel up and down his spine. Someone killed Mrs. Furry-paws. Someone had done this on purpose... but who?

4 Nine Street

"I don't know if this is a good idea," Eve said, sipping her tea. Having a guest stop by unexpected, or at all, wasn't something she was used to, even if it was a neighbour. Being asked to go out socially was completely unheard of. She was, in every respect, a shut-in.

Fellannie sighed. "We all know about your yearly problem..."

"Problem?" Eve interrupted. "I have no idea what you are referring to."

"Two words," Fellannie said over the top of a tea cup. Tiny pink flowers created a halo just under the rim of gold. It was almost too fancy to drink from, especially for an impromptu visit. The cup clattered as it found a familiar place on the matching saucer. "Toilet paper." Bits of cookie melted as it splashed into the still-steaming brew. What was left of the biscuit found its way between her lips. She'd brought them with her, already knowing her neighbour's reputation for being a health freak.

Eve's small frame shivered. "It isn't that big of a deal. I'm sure lots of houses in the area have a similar issue at that time of year."

"No," Fellannie disagreed. "They don't. You could try giving out candy instead of apples."

"Apples," Eve argued, "are nature's candy. They are just as much a treat as anything made from processed sugar and much better for kids. I really don't think that has anything to do with things. It's nothing more than the luck of the draw."

"You must be very unlucky," Fellannie scoffed. "They toilet paper your house every year. It would do you good to go out and have a bit of fun this year. Halloween doesn't have to be a bad word. Besides, Noah was good enough to provide us with two tickets to this magic show. He didn't do that for everyone around here, you know." She raised her eyebrows along with the tea cup.

Eve glanced at her sideways. "I suppose it would be a waste not to use them..."

"Perfect," Fellannie shrieked. "I'll drive. See you in about an hour, then?"

"Officer Rest!" Eve exclaimed, opening the door.

"Ma'am," the officer replied, removing his hat. "Sorry if I startled you. I was in the neighbourhood and thought I'd stop by to see if everything was okay."

"You know the night she needs you to stop by," Fellannie scoffed. "Why not make a pit stop then? Maybe you could protect her against those vandals for a change."

"I'd like nothing more, Ms. Cryme," the officer stated. "It's just that, Halloween is our busiest time. We can't afford to have a stake out for something that might not happen."

"Might not happen?" Fellannie argued. "It happens every year. It's a sure bet it will occur again this year the same way it has in the past. She deserves the protection of the force. Mark my words, something terrible is going to happen. I don't need to be a full-pledge psychic to know that."

"If it was up to me, I'd be sitting out front the whole week," the officer explained. "I have to follow orders, though."

"That's okay, Officer Rest," Eve said.

"Please, call me Al."

"Alright, Al," Eve replied, a pink blush surfacing on her cheeks.

"I'll try to check in as much as I can," Al offered.

"It's fine," Eve lied, waving her hand in front of her chest. "It's just a little toilet paper and some soap. That's hardly even a mess. I don't mind... really."

Fellannie rolled her eyes. "And I'm the Queen's mother. I guess Halloween is the season to pretend to be something we aren't."

*****

"Welcome to the most magical night of your lives!" the showman bellowed, his words echoing throughout the almost-empty auditorium.

A spotlight danced in circles before stopping directly on the magical man. Two clicks of his shiny black shoes and a ruffle of his long black jacket tails preceded a bow that included a flip of his top hat. When he came back up, a bouquet of plastic flowers appeared in one hand.

"Hold the applause," he commanded, not that there was any in the first place. "We have something special planned for you this evening. Unfortunately, my assistant is unable to be here."

Eve glanced around, unnerved by low grumbles. Moments later, they were replaced by the unmistakable sound of heavy doors slamming shut. The small crowd in attendance was thinning further.

"There is no need to be alarmed," the magician stated. "I'll have to ask for a volunteer. Would anyone like to be cut into two?"

A few gasps mingled with giggles. No one in their right mind would allow a second rate illusionist, with a box of tricks from a discount chain store, to saw them in half.

"No one?" the man pleaded. "How about a few volunteers to be hypnotized, then?"

A larger man snorted. "Alright! I'll prove you a fraud. Count me in." He waddled his way down to the stage, huffing after climbing the three steps. An already-used tissue emerged from one pocket to wipe the beads of sweat from his face and neck. They were out of control and quickly multiplying under the heat of the stage lights. Anything was a better option than letting them drip off his body to form a puddle at his feet.

"Anyone else?" the magician asked, shading his eyes from the brightness in an effort to see potential victims in the audience. "How about you?" He pointed to a teenage girl. "You." This time, his finger extended in the direction of a well-dressed young man. "And you."

Eve pointed to her own chest. "Me?"

"Yes, you," the magician replied. "Hurry up then. I need you all on stage." He motioned to an elderly man behind the fading red velvet drapes. The stage hand hurried out with a chair for each of the test subjects.

"Do we have to believe?" Eve asked in no more than a squeak.

"Believe?" the magician echoed. "My dear lady, absolutely not, but you will walk out of here a true believer. Mark my words." His fingers disappeared into the pocket of his silk vest, returning with a watch attached to a gold chain, tarnished and chipped in places. "Now, I want you all to concentrate. Look at the watch and follow its movements. Hear only my voice. I'm going to count back from ten and when I reach zero, you will be in a deep sleep.

"Ten. You are getting sleepy.

"Nine. You hear only the sound of my voice and the rhythm of your breathing. It soothes you.

"Eight. Your eyelids are starting to become heavy.

"Seven. The rhythm of your breathing soothes you like the sound of ocean waves crashing against rocks.

"Six. You can feel the weight of your eyelids. They slowly start to close.

"Five. You have no desire to fight the urge to fall asleep. Your arms and legs feel limp.

"Four. Your eyelids are too heavy to keep open. You are entering a deep sleep and can hear only the sound of my voice.

"Three. My voice calms you further. You are completely relaxed.

"Two. While you are asleep, you will answer to my voice and the instructions I have for you.

"One. When I snap once, you will be asleep. If I snap twice, you will awaken fully relaxed and refreshed with no memory of our session here today.

"Zero!" The magician snapped the fingers on his right hand.

The row of volunteers sat side-by-side, not one stirring.

"Right, then!" the magician stated. "I am talking to all of you at the moment. If I address an individual by name, only they will hear my words." He nodded towards the backstage. A lively tune started to play. He circled the four as if he were playing an unusual game of musical chairs, except nobody stood up when the song stopped. "Raise your right arm."

Each of the volunteers complied with the order.

"Excellent!" The magician said. "You can put it down now." He turned to the audience. "For this next part, I'll need to know something about each of our participants. Before you say anything, let me explain. I'd like to give them each a costume for Halloween. They won't just dress up as a character. They are

67

going to be whoever the rest of you choose. Doesn't that sound exciting?"

"Can you make him an attentive husband?!" a woman yelled, presumably the wife of the first volunteer.

A genuine laughter echoed through the hall - the first sign of anyone enjoying the evening. The magician joined in.

"I think we should try something a little less broad. How about a couple's costume? He could be a prince and you would be his princess in waiting. A little romantic nudge added in."

"If you can get Harv to agree to that, you really are a magician," the woman cackled.

The showman bowed down and whispered in Harv's ear, his lips curling up in a most mischievous manner as he spoke. The audience stretched and shifted, trying to see or hear something; anything. Whatever was spoken was between hypnotist and subject, no one else.

He pointed to Eve. "Who is with this lovely woman?"

"I am," Fellannie replied, waving. "She could use a boost of self-confidence, especially at this time of year. The poor girl brings it on herself, buying apples for the trick-or-treaters instead of candy. I'm sure you know kids can be ruthless. They toilet paper her house and soap the windows every year. If she could stand up for herself... chase them away."

"What's her name?" the magician asked.

"Eve," Fellannie answered. "Eve Ill."

He laughed. "That is too good to be true. I have the perfect costume - the evil, but beautiful queen from all the princess fairy tales. That will give her a good dose of attitude!"

Fellannie clapped her hands in agreement, tilting her head as she watched the man on stage whispering in her neighbour's ear.

After going through a similar process with the remaining two volunteers, he snapped his fingers twice. All four blinked several times, glancing around the room.

"I thought you were going to hypnotize us," Harv complained. "This is a pile of..."

"There are ladies in the room," the magician interrupted.

"He ain't no different!" Harv's wife yelled.

"I want a refund!" a man yelled. Most of the rest of the audience agreed, adding their grumbles into the mix.

Eve looked over her shoulder. She'd barely made it down the three stairs when the magician bolted, disappearing behind the curtains. There wasn't likely to be an encore that evening.

"How do you feel?" Fellannie asked.

"Fine," Eve said, glancing back one more time. "Funny, I didn't catch his name. Is it printed on the ticket?"

The snap on Fellannie's handbag clicked open. She examined the ticket stub, back to front. "No, it isn't. That's odd."

*****

Black coffee took a certain amount of courage to drink. The warm mug pressed to Eve's lips. They parted slightly, allowing the brown liquid to pass through. The first bitter taste awoke her senses, her eyes fully opening. She almost wished they hadn't after browsing through her closet. A new donation pile formed in the middle of her bedroom. She shook her head, throwing on the least offensive thing she could find. It was time to go shopping.

Eve bypassed her usual shopping haunts. She'd spent a lifetime saving every penny for a rainy day. That day had finally come and it was pouring. A thrift store wasn't going to satisfy her needs this time. It was fancy boutiques all the way.

Eve's hips swung wide with every step, her strut equivalent to what one might expect from a super model. Sunglasses balanced low on her nose, she glanced through the racks, looking for something that might tickle her fancy. A certain level of expectation reflected in her eyes.

"Can I help you find something?" a saleswoman asked.

Eve pulled down her sunglasses further, enough to give the woman a once over. She was dressed modestly so as not to offend those with more subtle tastes and still appeal to the more extravagant side of the elite. "I'm looking for a new style."

"Did you have something in mind?" the woman pried.

"Hm," Eve purred. "Form fitting, stylish and black."

The woman eyed her up and down. "Size?"

Eve laughed. She'd always worn clothes a little too large for her frame, hoping to hide anything and everything from view. Of course, it didn't help that most of the clothes she usually bought came only in sizes indicated by a letter rather than by a number. "Last time I checked, I was an eight. I might be able to squeeze into a six or seven though, depending on the fit."

"Very good," the woman replied. She fumbled through rack after rack before returning with a handful of choices. "The changing room is this way."

*****

Eve's arms threatened to break under the weight of the bags. New wardrobes were heavy and probably expensive. She hadn't looked at a single price tag or the totals before throwing down the credit card she'd had since she was eighteen. That poor card had spent every year of its existence locked away in a book safe on her shelf, waiting to be of use. No emergency had ever been big enough to break it free from its jail, until now. This was a fashion emergency.

She glanced in a mirror of a store passing by. Dressed in an all-black ensemble with high heels, she almost looked like a new person. There was only one thing missing. Eve glanced around, spotting a salon and spa a few paces away. It was time for a total makeover.

"Good afternoon," a woman at the front desk said. "How can I help you?"

Eve glanced over the services listed on the wall. "Hm. I want one of everything," she demanded.

"Excuse me?" the woman replied.

"I'd like one of everything," Eve repeated. "I'd like a cut, style and colour. I'd also like a manicure, pedicure, facial, makeup application and massage."

"Just one moment," the woman said, heading to the back and returning with a middle-aged man.

"Bonjour, madame," he said. "How are you? I'm Henry." The H remained silent.

"I'm doing fabulous," Eve replied. "Do you have time for me today?"

"For you," Henry said, "I will make time." He motioned for her to enter. "Do you know what you would like done?"

"Cut it off!" Eve ordered. A lifetime of long hair and tangles was coming to an end. "I want it short, spiky and black."

"Are you sure?" Henry questioned. "That is a drastic change from beautiful long locks."

"Yes, I am quite sure," Eve replied. "I'd like long nails as well, painted red. I've never been one for makeup, but I'd like to try something bold."

"As you wish," Henry replied, bowing. He snapped his fingers bringing over a crew of five to make all of her wishes come true.

*****

"It's 4 o'clock!" Andrew yelled over the intercom.

Eve had spent her life working at the same job in the same position for the same wage. Never once had she called in sick or been late.

"So it is," Eve replied.

"Well," Andrew complained. "Where have you been? You better make this good. I won't accept any lame excuses."

Eve pressed a button disconnecting the phone. She spun around in her chair twice before barging into her boss' office. "I went shopping," she declared.

Andrew eyed her up and down. "What have you done to yourself? You look more like a mistress of the night rather than my secretary. This behaviour is unacceptable."

"No," Eve scoffed. "Your behaviour is unacceptable. You are the very definition of a chauvinistic male pig, wanting to hold back every woman you meet. If it were up to you, you'd keep them locked under your thumb. For years, I've worked for you without respect or recognition. That little quiet mouse is now gone."

"You'd best be watching yourself," Andrew said, pushing himself back from his desk as far as possible. "You need this job."

Eve howled a laugh, ending it in a sinister grin. "Not as much as you need me. I am the one who knows all the passwords, where everything is filed and where you need to be. I'm the one who runs this place. You've been taking the credit, but that's coming to an end."

"Are you blackmailing me?" Andrew asked, loosening his tie.

"Not at all," Eve answered. "I'm quitting. Ta." She strutted out past the other workers with their ears pinned to the wall outside.

*****

Eve waved at Miss Demeanor glancing out from behind lace curtains. At least Fellannie was up-front and honest about being nosey. She swung her bags around, making sure to offer a quick view of the contents before dragging them inside to put away.

She looked at every item she purchased for a second time while unpacking them. A couple of bags of candy landed on the counter beside the apples, waiting for the sun to set. Even if she did switch things up and give out candy on Halloween, no one would know the night before. That was when the majority of damage was always done. Her reputation was the problem. Finding a way to rectify that wasn't going to be easy.

She glanced out her front window at a police car driving by slowly. Officer A. Rest was making his rounds. Unfortunately, that would be the last time she'd see him until the next day. It was understandable. Worse things happened on the night before Halloween than a little toilet paper. She shook her head. It was a lot of toilet paper. Nonetheless, it wasn't life threatening. Those cases needed to come first. What was a little soap and tissue compared to murder?

Her attention turned to her own hands. Thin fingers were graced by long nails with squared-off tips, each coated in a ruby red finish - the perfect accessory to any outfit. Nail extensions hadn't been as hard to become accustomed to as she had thought they would be. She wrapped each digit around a butcher's knife, as if their placement needed to be perfect.

A lack of nervousness formed as a partial smile on her lips. There was an exhilaration that attached itself to knowing she was about to do something she never had before - something she had considered taboo throughout most of her life. This was her moment.

She raised her hand, the blade catching a glimmer of light on its shiny surface, reflecting a twinkle back. She froze in that position for a moment, relishing the feeling of true power before the knife plummeted down into soft flesh. The tip moved in deeper, making a clean cut before pulling back out to make additional slashes. Each one was precise and calculated, made to allow for the removal of guts. Scooping them out was just as disgusting as she had imagined and yet somehow satisfying at the same time. She placed them in a bowl to patiently wait their disposal. It wasn't like anyone was going to complain. There was no one there to see the mess.

She gave her work the once over. "Not bad for my first time," she said. "Now to give you personality!" She picked up a marker and drew a face on one side of the pumpkin. A smaller blade made incisions along the lines, bringing a look of mischief and mayhem to life.

The lid on a soup pot danced as bubbles and steam escaped from wherever possible. Eve turned the heat down, the boiling water ready for the rest of her concoction. Rummaging through her cupboards, she added pinches of different items to the brew, humming as she worked. Everything needed to be perfect for the evening. This was her coming out party and she planned to throw a few kinks in the usual festivities.

A small table covered in black cloth was the first to appear on her porch. It wasn't anything new; she'd given up answering the door for trick-or-treaters years ago after being hit by a few stray rotten eggs. The odour had stayed on her for weeks, intensified by shame. Children knew how to be cruel in ways adults could never comprehend. After that, she decided it was easier to simply make a display for them to help themselves.

Decorations were new this year. Being an introvert most of her life, Eve never wanted to draw attention to herself. Elaborate celebrations were meant to do just that. Nobody hosted a party hoping not to be noticed. This year, she was throwing caution to the wind. Cobwebs tangled with hanging chains, creating a spooky wind chime, warning those approaching to turn around. If that wasn't enough, she placed several signs around the large tree in her front yard demanding trespassers turn back before it was too late.

Time passed quickly. The sun began its final descent, going down in a blaze of orange glory that mimicked the flickering lights inside her carved pumpkins. It wasn't Halloween yet, but tonight was about making a statement. She placed a bowl of candy on the table with a sign: *Take At Your Own Risk*. One red nail tapped above her upper lip. Eve retreated inside, returning with a basket of perfectly shiny red apples. She'd given them the choice, hoping they'd make the right one. All there was left to do was wait. As soon as the last rays of light disappeared, they'd come.

She crouched low on her couch, peeking around the curtains to see if her plan was working. A barrage of eggs hit the outside of the glass, sending her shrinking down further to remain hidden.

"Too little, too late," a boy called, followed by a round of laughter.

Eve remained still, waiting for them to pass. If they knew she was watching or listening, they would have acted out all the more. No one would help her if mischief and vandalism turned more violent. As long as she was the target, no one else was. That was what society had come to - looking out for number one.

After fifteen minutes of silence had passed, her courage returned. She peeked out the curtains again. They were gone and along with them the candy, bowl and all. As for her yard, it was too dark to assess the damage. Turning on a light now might draw attention back to her home. It was better to wait the night and clean up in the morning.

*****

Eve glanced around the yard. A squirrel feasting on bits of smashed pumpkin paid no attention to her. Its tiny hand-like paws held chunks in place while its front teeth gnawed off bits, stuffing as much as possible into its mouth. Air filled her own cheeks, mimicking the tiny animal less than ten feet away, making a hissing sound as it slowly escaped closed lips.

The smashed pumpkins were only part of the problem. There were broken eggs and what looked like human feces all over. Keeping with the theme, toilet paper clung to branches of her tree and decorated smaller bushes.

She grabbed the garden hose, scaring away any creature trying to scavenge a free meal, including the squirrel. The car had taken the brunt of the attack and needed attention first. She sighed. A layer of grit and grime covered every window. The words *WASH ME* were written in numerous places, as if dirt was finger paint. She set the water blast to its strongest spray and took aim. Plain water barely made a dent in the mixture. Still, she let it rinse whatever it could off. The less she had to scrub by hand, the better.

A police car pulled out of her neighbour's driveway. She tilted her head from side to side, wondering why Officer A. Rest was at Fellannie's. One hand smoothed her hair as his car pull up to the curb.

"Good morning, Eve," Al said. "Had some trouble here last night, I see."

"I have trouble every year," Ever snapped back. "You know that. This year was particularly bad."

"I can see that," Al commented. "Did you have some sort of an unusual run-in with them?"

"Obviously," Eve replied. Turning off the water, she threw the hose down. "I don't suppose you have enough proof to catch them this year."

"What time were they here?" the officer asked, pulling out a notebook and scribbling down information.

"Why the sudden interest?" Eve questioned. "You say every year that nothing can be done, even though we know who is responsible."

"Except this year," the officer explained, "those you accuse year after year are in the hospital. It's the damnedest thing I ever did see. The lot of them... all in a coma. The doctor says it's a poison of some sort, but no one knows which one."

"What's that got to do with me?" Eve asked.

"You had motive," Al replied.

"Are you kidding me?" Eve squealed. "I'm a victim. I never do anything, but sit in my house and let that bunch walk all over me like everyone else around here. Now this?" She threw her arms in the air.

"Yes ma'am, I know." Al stated. "Except this year, you have been acting different. I talked to your work and seems you up and quit. That's not the Eve I know."

"What does one have to do with the other?" Eve complained.

"Well, I got to talking with your neighbour," Al said. "She says you attended a hypnosis show... that you went under and it was suggested to you that you might be a villain from one of those fairy tales." He walked to her front porch and nodded at the basket of apples. "I have a bunch of teens in a coma and the last person they saw was a woman hypnotized into believing she was an evil queen with a basket of apples."

"Are you suggesting I poisoned the apples?" Eve asked, adding a cackle to the end of her words. Her fingers eagerly snatched up one of the fruits. Locking her eyes on his, her teeth sunk into the red skin with a crunch, extracting juices that couldn't be contained. They trickled down from the corners of her lips. She smiled, finishing the mouthful with a gulp. "Still alive."

Al nodded his head. "It's my job to ask." he explained. "I'll have to take the rest of these."

"Be my guest," Eve said. She walked inside, slamming the door behind her.

3 Nine Street

This year, the seasons were playing a game. In the field of battle, each wanted to arrive sooner and leave later. Fall had made an early appearance, then disappeared again, as if chased off. Now, it was late; frightened to show its face, but peeking round the corner to see if the coast was clear. The colour on the trees had transformed from green into those that radiated the warmth of a raging fire, yet the leaves themselves remained intact - moisture having been sealed in by Mother Nature's wax. The usual crunch under shoes of fallen leaves, crisp and crinkly, was non-existent. The grass clung to vibrant green tones, still requiring a once-a-week cut - a task well worth the extra work for the extended warm temperatures.

Fellannie inhaled deeply, filling her lungs with the crisp air. A chill nipped at her nose, letting her know summer had lost the latest round and was in retreat. It could have happened at any moment. One frigid day was all it would take to steal life from the last of the holdouts, sending warmth into memories and much of nature to slumber. A triangle of birds flew overhead, preparing to vacate until spring. They wouldn't stop, not now. Nine Street was the last place anything wanted to be lately.

She glanced from side to side at the empty road. There had been a shift in activity since Noah's dinner. At first, she chalked it up to having an overactive imagination. Now, she questioned whether her intuition might have been correct.

While some neighbours were satisfied watching from behind closed curtains and remaining in the shadows, this street's resident busy-body needed more. That was Fellannie Cryme's department. Unlike the other nosey neighbour, Miss Demeanor, who preferred the peeping-Tom approach, she inserted herself directly into the action. Because of that, she knew everyone and everything that happened on Nine Street, or at least she liked to believe she did. Keeping that status meant staying active.

First thing in the morning, there was nothing better than an early yoga session on her front lawn. From there, she appeared preoccupied and yet still had a birds-eye view of all. Of course, something had to happen for her to have a view of it. The only information she'd found out recently was leaked by the police.

That was her focus. She was determined to find out what Eve was being investigated for. Positioning was the key to her success. Picking the perfect angle, she dropped down to the ground.

A mat of vibrant colours cushioned her bottom as arms and legs contorted into different positions aimed at stretching every muscle possible. The session always ended the same - in an upright sitting position; legs criss-crossed. Her hands were together in front of her chest; palms touching as if praying. Of course, she wasn't. Keeping her eyes closed and mind open allowed for better hearing. On numerous occasions, she had picked up bits of information whispered on the wind from that strategy. No one paid attention to someone who was focused, deep in meditation.

"Excuse me," a mouse of a voice said.

Two words were enough to completely decimate Fellannie's theory. She revised her previous summation: *No normal individual paid attention or disturbed someone who was meditating.*

One eye popped open. "Claire," Fellannie replied, wiggling her shoulders. "What can I do for you?" She re-closed the eye, confident she had been correct and wasn't dealing with a normal person.

"I was hoping to borrow a cup of sugar," Claire said, shaking an empty cup in front of her.

Fellannie stuck a single finger out. She inhaled deeply ten times, before bending at the waist, her nose touching the mat. Sitting back up, she smiled, offering her neighbour her full attention. "A cup of sugar?"

Claire Voyant was notorious for running out of different things on a daily basis. Normally, however, she asked her other neighbours. "I thought I had another bag in the cupboard and I am in the middle of baking. It would be ever so helpful if I could borrow some."

"Of course," Fellannie replied, jumping to her feet and regretting the quick movement. She wasn't used to being lightheaded. The intensity of the world spinning out of control and a desperate need to be back on the ground again made her feel as if she was drowning. She shook her head, trying to reclaim her bearings. A few blinks and deep breaths were enough to subside whatever it was she had just experienced. "I'll be right back." She snatched the cup from her neighbour's hand.

The glass container sat on the kitchen counter. Fellannie rubbed her fingers together, trying to outsmart the numbness trying to sneak in and take hold of one of her most important senses - touch. The weight of the bag of sugar surprised her, falling to the counter while still in her grasp. She took a step back. It had to be a drastic misalignment in her core. There was no other explanation.

Summoning all of her focus, she lifted the bag again, pouring a steady stream of the sweet white powder. Only half found its way into Claire's cup; the rest lay in a pile on the counter beside it.

Fellannie bent at the waist, taking a better look at how much sugar actually missed the mark. The gold chain around her neck came free from its usual home, resting against bare skin beneath her shirt. A small circular talisman dangled off the bottom, performing its own ritual of protection against all things evil.

A tug jolted her head downwards. Grasping the medallion in one hand to try to alleviate its new-found weight wasn't enough. She might as well have been wearing a cinder block on her chest while trying to swim. Both hands joined the struggle. She wasn't about to go down without a fight. As fast as it started, it was over. Her feet tangled trying to balance with the heaviness now gone, sending her into a backwards stumble - the sink becoming her saviour, providing enough support to avoid an entire wipeout.

Preoccupied with her own state, she returned to her neighbour patiently waiting at the door. "Here you go," she said, almost dropping the container. Fellannie gasped.

"Is everything alright?" Claire asked.

"Fine," Fellannie lied, an obviously fake part-smile coming and going quickly. Her hand reached for the necklace, now warm to the touch. The heat increased with every passing second, her skin blistering without notice. Her gaze was drawn to Claire. Once locked, she couldn't look away. It had only been a minute or two since the woman had been left standing there, but her appearance had completely altered. "Goodbye." She closed the door all but a crack, watching her neighbour walk away... on her hands.

Fellannie let out a squeak. Using the back of her hand as a thermometer, she eliminated the chance that a fever was to blame for the hallucinations. She pinched the bridge of her nose, wondering what she would do if everyone outside had arms for legs and legs for arms.

*****

"Come in, Fellannie," a woman said, from behind a door made entirely of strings of beads. "You sounded upset on the phone. What brings you in today?"

Fellannie let out the breath of air she had been holding in for a little too long. "I think I might be seeing things," she stated. "Perhaps even losing my mind, Sue."

"Have a seat and I'll draw a card for you," Sue offered. She poured tea into a small handle-less cup, setting it in front of her guest. Soothing notes rang out as she moved, the result of tiny bells attached to a piece of sheer black material tied around her midsection. It added a new dimension to the woman's layered clothes, sitting high on one side and low on the other, mimicking a hip belt.

"I am not sure that will help," Fellannie replied, wringing her scarf into a twisted ball of knots. "This is bad."

"I see that," Sue replied, placing cards face up on the table between them. "There is an energy around you that isn't good. My sight is blurred from whatever it is."

"Oh," Fellannie cried. "What do I do?"

"Tell me what you have been seeing," Sue ordered.

"People," Fellannie started, gulping back a mouthful of the tea meant to be sipped. "They act normal, but I see them with their arms and legs in the opposite spots."

"Do you see me like that?' Sue asked.

"No," Fellannie admitted.

"Where does this happen? Is it restricted to one place?" A heavy scent of sage filled the air, eliminating any impurities that might have tried to hitch a ride, entering the room without invitation. The candle beside them lit, its flame joining the party.

"Yes," Fellannie replied. "I suppose it is only neighbours on my street. What can that mean?"

"Something happened recently," Sue said, her eyes closed and hand hovering above the cards. "You had a meeting or get-together. That's when all of this began. That night, something was put in motion. Whatever it is, I don't think anything good can come of it."

"Yes!" Fellannie exclaimed, sitting on the very edge of her seat. "What else do you see?"

"Sometimes, our visions can have a rather simple and obvious meaning," Sue explained, turning the now empty tea cup upside down. "In yours, your neighbours' limbs appear in the wrong places. What is one word that comes to mind for that?"

"Backwards," Fellannie replied.

"Exactly," Sue said. "Take whatever was said at that meeting and believe the opposite to be true. That is my advice for you." She looked inside the cup at the diagram left by remaining tea leaves. "Once you do, things will return to normal."

2 Nine Street

There was nothing worse than starting to bake and finding out there wasn't enough of one item or another in her pantry. Of course, baking a lot meant it happened a lot. Usually, borrowing a cup of sugar was easier. Lately, however, there had been an absence of presence. They lived on a fairly quiet dead end street, but it had never been completely silent in the morning.

Claire hopped over a small hedge, taking a minute to look at the Mr. And Mrs. Rhe's yard. They'd been digging and planting for weeks now and it still looked as unfinished as the day they started. There were holes with trees and plants waiting to go in them, a pile of dirt and a wide array of garden tools, all littering the front lawn. Normally, the couple would have been up taking advantage of the sunlight while it was available. It didn't make sense that the days were getting shorter and they were getting started later. At the rate the pair was going, they were destined to be planting well after the first snow fall. Not the best idea, at least from any plant's point of view.

She stumbled, almost losing her balance, precious sugar falling from the container she held - a rake was to blame. She mumbled under her breath about people leaving things lying around. Such carelessness was a hazard. It didn't matter that she didn't have the right to be in their yard in the first place.

Her breath and heart stopped, one eye catching an odd movement from the side. The rake had wiggled on its own. She complained about it and it moved. But how? That wasn't possible. There wasn't anyone around. She glanced at the tool again, wavy lines appearing all around it. She shook her head, wondering if she was stuck in an odd dream. A pinch provided the probable answer to that question. It hurt, leaving a red mark on her arm. There was a good chance what she was experiencing was real.

She slowly stepped backwards, almost tripping over the hedge. Nothing was going to make her look away and miss something else. One leg lifted then the other. She was safely back on the sidewalk again. The rake jolted again. This time she knew she had seen it.

Claire inhaled deeply, filling her lungs for the quick jog home. She bent over sharply, stricken by a cough - not the usual type resulting from a cold. This cough was trying to rid her body of the putrid air that it had sucked in. Rotten eggs weren't foul enough to describe the odour. Death had interwoven itself with that which provided life - the two now inseparable. Her only chance was to make it to her house away from the foul stench. Her legs made strides even before the thought was finished. White powder lay in a mound on the ground - the sugar she had gone out of her way to borrow now forgotten. A breeze picked up the granules, distributing them as if destroying evidence of a crime.

Claire tugged on her door, throwing it open. "Phew," she sighed, plopping down on her couch. She lifted her legs, reclining into a laying position. Breathing was all she wanted to do.

"This can't be real," she told herself. "Things don't move on their own."

What if you moved it? A voice in her head answered back.

She sat up straight. Could she have moved the rake? She had been thinking about just that at the exact moment it happened. There were reported cases all over the world of people who could do extraordinary things with their minds.

"I need a sign," Claire said. Her eyelids twitched under the pressure of concentration. "If I can do things, if I can move things with my mind, show me a sign!"

Nothing happened. Her tongue darted out, leaving a layer of moisture on her lips - a replacement for what the wind had stolen earlier.

"Stupid!" she complained, slapping the palm of her hand to her forehead. She lifted her gaze to the ceiling, then lowered it again - the corner of her eye catching a shadow darting across the floor.

Claire stood, following the direction of whatever it had been. The sound of a plate shifting in the next room made her jump backwards. Was this her sign? She had been thinking about getting the dishes done earlier.

The kitchen sat in a state of disarray, the mess from baking scattered around counters and tables. Claire gingerly made her way past one pile to another, looking for which the noise had come from, but finding nothing.

There was no explanation for what she was experiencing. None, that is, except that she had the gift - the power to move things with her mind.

She clapped her hands together, letting out a squeal of delight. All her life she'd wanted a superhero power. Now she had one.

She glanced around at the state of her kitchen. Superhero or not, her new-found ability was draining her energy. She needed a nap, clean up would have to wait until later.

1 Nine Street

Victor reached out from under his covers, one hand swatting at the clock, hoping to blindly hit the snooze button. It failed. His legs swung around, dragging the rest of his body into an upright position, feet touching down into awaiting slippers. The alarm silenced. His hand returned with a white plastic bottle. The lid popped off with a flick of his thumb. He chugged back the contents like he was drinking a beer.

"That's not good for you," Jewel complained.

"Neither is this headache," he retorted, glancing at the digital numbers coming into focus. "Geez, did we sleep in again? It's a good thing I took two weeks off. I wouldn't have a job getting up this late every day."

"As I recall, you took the time off to finish the front yard," his wife stated, starting to stir under the comforter. "The days are getting shorter and the list of things to be done, longer."

"I don't see you getting up any earlier than me," Victor said, yawning.

"I know," Jewel agreed. "It's been worrying me. Maybe we should start a new vitamin program... get our energy levels up."

Victor rolled his eyes. "Next you'll be having us do yoga outside with the neighbour. No, thank you. It's probably just the weather changing. By this time next week, we'll be back to normal."

"Uh-huh," Jewel replied. "If you think so. Do you want breakfast?"

"Breakfast," Victor snorted. "It's almost time for dinner. I'll take a pass. I better get to work. Those trees and bushes you bought aren't going to plant themselves."

"Next time maybe you'll listen and let me hire a landscaper to do the job," Jewel commented.

"And waste all that money?" her husband argued.

*****

Victor whistled at the amount of work left to do - much more than he remembered. Greenery in all shapes and sizes littered the lawn, waiting for their new home. Jewel had chosen the spots. Now it was up to him to put them in properly.

He loosened the sacking attached to the roots of the first ornamental tree and measured for the approximate depth required. If he was wrong, it would never make it through the winter and he'd end up spending his holidays next year replanting the whole yard. It was bad enough he had to do weeding and upkeep annually.

The metal of the shovel sank into the ground, prying up the top layer of turf and dirt. It slammed down in an overflowing wheelbarrow still waiting to be emptied from the day before. His foot came down on the edge of the shovel, driving it further in. It wasn't the first hole to be dug, but it also wasn't anywhere near the last.

His sleeve mopped up the sweat from his brow. Digging had been only half the equation. Dragging the trees to their new homes was heavy lifting his back wasn't used to. Muscles had found their voices and were screaming for relief.

Other lawyers hired people to do the dirty work and concentrated on winning cases or improving their golf scores. He couldn't bring himself to waste the money, paying someone for something he could do himself. Maybe one day he would, when he was a partner in a major law firm and making the big bucks. Right now, he was merely a member of the staff where he worked - only a step above secretary and paid only slightly better than one.

He tossed shovelfuls of dirt over the roots, making sure they were evenly coated and protected from the looming first frost. Trees were the most important in his mind. They were also the most expensive to replace. The afternoon flew by, chock-full of digging holes and filling them up again, a game that as a young lad he had enjoyed. That wasn't the case anymore. Losing his balance, he stumbled backwards, narrowly escaping a fall on his backside. He shook the cobwebs from his head. A combination of exhaustion, stress, heat and hunger fought amongst themselves for which had the right to claim responsibility for his dizziness. Whichever it was didn't matter, Victor was listening. A short break for diner was in order.

*****

Victor rubbed the back of his neck. Taking the break had cleared his head, but the sun was beginning its descent and he was nowhere near finished for the night.

He squatted down to pick up the shovel. There was no use aggravating his back muscles any more than they already were by bending improperly. A glance over his shoulder confirmed his wife was watching his every move from the porch, ready to pounce if he did something wrong.

The shovel didn't have time to hit the ground before he wobbled. This time, it wasn't his head throwing him off-balance. The ground itself had rumbled. He took a step back to the driveway, standing on the paved surface.

"Did you see that?" he called to his wife.

"See what?"

"The ground moved!" Victor exclaimed. "It could have been an earthquake."

"I think you may have hurt more than your back," Jewel answered. "Maybe you should stop work for the night."

"Sh," Victor mouthed. "There." He pointed at a patch of newly-laid grass.

A gurgling sound accompanied a movement under the turf. It changed to a grinding noise, one only older pipes in a house tended to make. The spot began to shift, before cracking open with a loud bang. A thick white fog escaped from the crevice now dividing the Rhe's lawn.

Jewel screamed, her body shaking. "What was that? Something came out of that hole."

"Where?" Victor asked, straining to see through the mist.

"Over there!" Jewel yelled, pointing at a bunch of bushes.

"I don't see anything..." Victor announced, his words trailing off. "What is that?" He ran to his wife's side.

"What is what?" Fellannie asked, the first neighbour to make an appearance. "What did you do to your lawn?"

"We didn't do anything," Jewel replied. "That thing with the yellow eyes burst out of the ground. It's over there in the bushes."

"I don't see anything," Fellannie stated, giving the entire area a once over.

"What happened?" Claire asked.

"I think we should wait for them," Fellannie replied, nodding towards the other neighbours making their way towards them.

"What a mess!" Miss Demeanor exclaimed. "Seems whatever you were trying to bury didn't agree with being left to rot."

"What is that supposed to mean?!" Victor yelled, his nostrils flaring. "If you are trying to accuse me of something, come out and say it."

"It did smell like death here earlier," Claire stated.

"Doesn't smell much better now," Eve added.

A sudden blast of a siren caught their attention first. Flashing lights grew stronger as the last rays of sunlight disappeared. The yellow tinted headlights of more than one vehicle shone directly at them, illuminating the scene. After a few moments, an officer stepped out, flashlight in hand.

"What's going on here?" Officer A. Rest asked. "Complaints are coming in from several blocks away. Frankly, I'm bewildered as to the number of visits I've had to make to this street in the past few weeks." He shone a light at the crevice, motioning for other officers to join him.

"It was..."

Al held up a hand. "Not now. I'll talk to you all back at the station. Bessy will give you a ride over. You best listen to her until I get done here."

"Okay, folks," Bessy bellowed. "It isn't a limo ride, but it will have to do." She opened the back of a police van, motioning for them to find a seat inside.

Before the doors closed, they heard Al asking the other officers to set up a perimeter and block off the area. Something was definitely wrong on Nine Street.

9th Precinct Police Department

"This way," an officer said, holding open one of the glass doors leading to the main lobby of the local police department.

"Where are we going?" Fellannie asked. She gauged the thickness of the glass, wondering if it was bulletproof or if there was any need for it to be.

The intake room itself was anything but comfortable - made to process whoever and whatever came in quickly. No thought whatsoever had gone into creating an enjoyable stay. Wooden benches lined the walls, cold and hard. In a word, they were criminal. To sit for any length of time on one would be agonizing for any bottom. That didn't take into account the germs that had hopped off the last person to sit there, now festering - lying in wait on an old piece of gum stuck to the underside for an unsuspecting victim to latch onto.

"We need a room," Bessie said, motioning with her head at her haul of persons of interest.

A tall desk took up much of the wall directly in front of the doors. An officer looked up at Bessie, then at the group in tow. He nodded silently, a buzzer being used to replace any words he might have needed to say.

"This way," Bessie directed, opening a side door leading to offices. She glanced in and waved at every open room they passed, heading to the back of the building and a staircase leading up.

"Don't you have elevators?" Fellannie complained.

"We sure do," Bessie replied. "I've been doing the healthy choice challenge. That means I take the stairs instead of a ride up. It's been doing wonders for my cellulite. You should try it." She chuckled. "Guess you don't have a choice today."

Fellannie bit her tongue. If they were already in trouble, which she was sure they were, aggravating a police officer wasn't going to help.

"Right in here," Bessy directed, opening a door.

"You have to be kidding," Fellannie barked. The room was right out of a bad detective movie. "What shade of grey is this, prison cell?" She fixed her hair in the large mirror taking up a vast majority of one of the four walls, blowing a kiss to her image and whoever might be watching from the other side after finishing.

"Take a seat," Bessy ordered. "Al will be with you shortly."

"This isn't right," Victor complained.

"So do something," Fellannie suggested. "Last I checked, you were the only lawyer in the room."

Victor pursed his lips together, his nostrils flaring each time he exhaled. "I don't actually practice criminal law," he mumbled.

"What law do you practice?" Miss Demeanor asked, taking a seat on a cold, grey metal chair.

"Family law," Victor admitted, shrugging his shoulders. "If anyone is in need of a divorce..."

"Well, that's helpful," Fellannie scoffed. "Maybe you should have thought of that before blowing up your lawn."

"Blowing up," Victor complained. "I did no such thing."

"It was to hide the evidence, I tell you," Miss Demeanor spat out. "He buried something out there."

"I didn't bury anything," Victor argued, sweat forming on his brow. "I wish people would stop saying that."

"We shouldn't jump to conclusions," Eve suggested.

"You are probably in league with him," Fellannie said. "The police were sniffing around about whatever happened the other night between you and those kids."

"Enough!" Al bellowed from the door way. He slammed it shut, tossing a file on the smooth surface of the metal table. "Have a seat."

"Officer," Miss Demeanor said. "I'd like to report a crime."

"I'm sure you would," Al replied. "Let's handle one incident at a time. I've just come back from Nine Street and I can report Mr. Rhe hit a gas line while digging. If any of you feel sick, dizzy or nauseous, it's straight to the hospital to get checked out. Anyone?" He paused for a moment, glancing from person to person. "Alright then, let's proceed. Mr. Rhe, do you have anything to add?"

"It wasn't a gas line," Jewel Rhe interrupted. "I saw something crawl out. It looked like a large black shadow with yellow eyes. I'll never forget that icy-cold stare."

Al bounced his pencil, eraser side down, on the table. "Gas, when inhaled, can do funny things to our bodies." he suggested. "It plays tricks on our minds. I assure you this is a case of a bad leak. The gas company is there right now fixing it. No one has mentioned any creatures lurking about."

"What about my cat?" Vic asked. "Mrs. Furry-paws has been missing for days. And I found this note." He dropped the piece of torn paper on the table.

"Why would anyone want to kill your cat?" Al asked.

"I tried to tell you I wanted to report a crime," Miss Demeanor said. "You didn't want to listen."

"Alright," Al replied. "I'm listening now."

"Those two did it," Miss Demeanor said, pointing at Mr. And Mrs. Rhe. "I was enjoying a cup of tea before bed when I saw them."

Vic gasped, his mouth hanging open.

"You mean you were spying on us," Jewel complained. "Why would we kill a cat? This is ridiculous."

"It was some sick ritual," Miss Demeanor stated.

"What exactly did you see?" Al asked.

"The blinds were down, but I still saw them," Miss Demeanor explained. "Two silhouettes stabbing a cat. Blood splattered everywhere. It frightened me half to death. I couldn't sleep a wink."

"Oh, for crying out loud," Victor said. "There was no cat murdering happening. I can explain this. Jewel wanted one of those Halloween projectors."

"Victor thought he could save a few bucks, like he always does," Jewel started.

"It was a good deal," Victor argued.

"It's only a good deal if we can use it," Jewel complained. "When we turned it on, it had the most frightening scenes, one of which was exactly what Miss Demeanor described. I had him throw it out right away. I wanted to be the cool house on the block, not the demented one." She rolled her eyes at her husband.

"That still doesn't explain what happened to Mrs. Furrypaws," Vic blurted out.

"If you ask me," Eve said, "this is all started after we had dinner with No Body. He's the one to blame."

Al shook his head. "Who is to blame?"

"No Body," Eve repeated.

"Nobody is to blame," Al said.

"Not nobody," Fellannie interrupted. "No Body."

"Well, that certainly makes it clear," Al said, raising his eyebrows.

Fellannie let out a huff. "Noah Body, he owns Nine, Nine Street. He had all of us over for dinner to tell us about a curse. Honestly, you are the detective. Don't you get paid to know these things?"

"Not exactly," Al replied. "I'd like to meet this Mr. Body."

"Good," Bessy said from the door. "Cause he's right here. He showed up at the site, insisting on being part and parcel to this discussion. One of the boys dropped him off. They might have been tired of listening to him ramble on. I know I am."

"Good evening, Officer," Noah said, ignoring his escort. "I think I can clear up a great deal of the problem."

"Well," Al replied, "I'm certainly glad someone can." He motioned to Bessy to close the door, receiving an eye-roll as a reply before it shut.

"Yes," Noah said. "I am an entrepreneur with a particular taste for the unusual. When I saw Nine, Nine street up for grabs, I thought it would be a good investment."

"What exactly are you in the business of?" Al asked.

"Restaurants, hotels, retreats - all with a flair for the supernatural," Noah explained. "The history behind Nine Street made for a perfect backdrop; one I couldn't bring myself to let slip by."

"But nobody knew about the street's sordid past," Al commented.

"Exactly," Noah admitted. "I needed the word to be spread and I needed it to be believable."

"So you staged a dinner party to plant the thought of this curse in the minds of the neighbours," Al suggested.

"It wouldn't be a very good curse if no one on the street knew about it," Noah offered. "I never expected it to come to this."

"You expect us to believe that," Fellannie scoffed. "What about Maggie? No one has heard from her since the dinner party."

Al sucked in a breath of air. "I can explain that," he replied. "The man she was engaged to was killed in a fluke accident. I'm sure you saw the news crews hanging around for a few days. Maggie sent messages to everyone important in her life saying she wanted space and wouldn't be around for a while. I doubt anyone will hear from her until she finishes grieving. Maggie isn't missing, she doesn't want to be found and those that love her the most understand that. If they aren't trying to find her, I don't think any of you should be either."

"Okay," Fellannie said, colour rising in her face. "What about Eve? I know you were investigating her. It had something to do with the kids that vandalized her home. I heard they were hospitalized."

Miss Demeanor gasped.

"It's true," Fellannie continued. "I bet it was poison. She was hypnotized, you know. I was there."

"I faked it," Eve blurted out. "I faked the whole thing. I was never under any spell and I never thought I was some evil queen."

"Why?" Al asked.

Eve's eyes watered. Her top teeth covered her bottom lip. "I spent my whole life being the person no one noticed. I was a door mat and tired of having people use me to wipe their feet on." She sniffled, extending her neck to hold her head high. "It isn't easy to change, you know. If you do it subtly no one notices or, if they do, they dismiss it. It seemed, at the time, this gave me the perfect way to change my life around." She pulled down a sleeve, using it for a tissue.

"You quit your job," Al stated.

"I know," Eve said, half-laughing and half-crying at the same time. "But my boss called and asked me to come back at twice the salary and better hours. I agreed, of course. I'm not crazy, just reinventing."

"What about the kids?" Fellannie questioned.

"It turns out there is this crazy online challenge," Al replied. "Eating laundry detergent, of all things. There are a slew of kids with the same symptoms in hospitals all across the country. I don't get it, but that is what we determined happened." He paused. "Besides, we ran a test on the apples. They came up clean."

"Did you test the candy too?" Miss Demeanor asked.

"What candy?" Eve questioned.

"I saw you." Miss Demeanor waggled a finger in Eve's direction. "Bringing in your groceries from the store. There were a few bags of candy hidden in them. What did you do with those?"

"Everyone knows I don't buy candy," Eve argued. "I don't know what you saw, but you were mistaken. You know we've all been sharing, but I haven't heard what happened to Fellannie or Claire."

"I didn't want to boast," Claire stated, "but I have a super power. I can move things with my mind."

"Really," Al said. "Can you move this pencil for me?"

"Of course." Claire wiggled her bottom in the chair before focusing her attention on the pencil, lying perfectly still on the table. Her lips disappeared, pressed tightly together. The colour of her face turned from pink to red within moments. Nothing happened.

Al raised his hand. "I think that is enough. I'd like you to consider the possibility that the gas leak might have affected you on a slightly higher level than you may realize."

Claire frowned, her gaze still locked on the pencil. "Guess it's your turn, Fellannie."

Fellannie chuckled. "I'm not sure I should be sharing this information with the present company," she stated, fixing a stare in Mr. Body's direction. "I had a vision, and a quite profound one at that."

Al nodded. "What was in this vision?"

"Everyone on Nine Street had their arms and legs reversed," she declared. "I saw my spiritual adviser to confirm the meaning. We both agreed that I should take Noah Body's words as a complete opposite to the truth."

"Okay. I suppose that could be one explanation," Al replied. "The gas leak could be another, though." He looked around the room. "I think everything that has happened has a plausible explanation - one that doesn't involve otherworldly curses. That's what I am putting in my report. As soon as the gas company says it is okay, I'll arrange transportation for you all back."

"Mrs. Furry-paws is still missing," Vic cried, "and what about the note?"

"Can I see that?" Claire asked, reaching across the table. "I know I've seen this before somewhere. *I killed your*... where did I see that?" Her eyes stared at the ceiling, mouth twitching from side to side.

"It certainly doesn't look like a typical death note," Eve suggested.

"How many death notes have you seen?" Fellannie blurted out. "I'll answer that, none. No one here has. We aren't common criminals. The notes we see are reminders of the groceries we need to pick up from the store. We are more likely to receive a coupon than a death threat."

"That's it," Claire said, snapping her fingers. "*I killed your pests!* It was in the coupon book that came in the mail for the pest control guy. You must have torn it up and drop a piece... this piece." She held the scrap high for everyone to see, her face glowing. Sleuthing had just become her second super power.

"Yes," Vic admitted. "I guess it could have happened that way. That doesn't change the fact the Mrs. Furry-paws is still missing."

"We'll keep looking," Al promised.

*****

A caged animal was what she had been reduced to. Sitting in the back of the car, she might as well have had handcuffs on.

The black interior was bad enough, but the moment the doors locked, she was trapped. Metal grating stood between her and Officer Rest. He could step out of his own free will. She, however, was on the wrong side.

Thoughts accelerated in her head, she needed to escape. Her heart pounded, a hammer hitting a nail over and over; faster and faster. Her mouth opened but no words would form. She was drowning, without water. There simply wasn't any air. Her lungs were starving.

"Looks like the power isn't back on yet," Al said.

Eve nodded, feeling the tension in her chest begin to vacate - home was in sight, even if it was pitch dark.

"Officer Rest," a voice said over the CB radio. "Mr. Body has suggested they convene at his place. Apparently, he has a generator and a rather large candle supply they can use until the power is restored."

"Copy that," Al replied. "We'll meet out front."

The flashing lights weren't enough to cut through the night, merely casting shadows that further fuelled the fear already circulating amongst them. Even with all the explanations, doubt was firmly planted in each of their minds.

"Perhaps we should wait until the lights come back on," Fellannie suggested, shivering. She took her place with her neighbours, lined up like a bunch of criminals waiting to be identified.

"You'll feel better once I have the generator running," Noah suggested. "Light cures all."

"I don't think I'll be feeling better anytime soon," Miss Demeanor muttered.

"We've gone over all this," Al announced. "There is nothing to be afraid of. Everything has been explained."

"Not everything," Fellannie said, nodding at Eight, Nine Street. "We haven't seen hide nor hair of the couple that moved in there. What happened to them?"

The group all glanced over their shoulders at the still house. A light turned on in the uppermost window, the silhouette of a woman making a graceful appearance as if overseeing the unfolding events.

"Looks to me like everything over there is fine," Al snickered.

"How do you explain the fact they have power when none of us do?" Fellannie argued.

"They most likely have their own generator," Noah suggested. "It isn't as uncommon as you might think."

"Aren't you even going to go check things out?" Fellannie shrieked. "Isn't it your job to make sure things are okay?"

"What would you like me to say?" Al asked. "There have been no missing person reports and I can clearly see someone in the window. There is no reason for me to disturb them."

Fellannie threw her arms in the air and let them fall back down. "Fine. It's getting cold out here, can we hurry this up?"

A smile crept over Noah's face, one of a man who'd won in battle. His attention reverted to the locks, each one squeaking as if being tortured, before admitting defeat and opening. The clatter of the heavy chains and padlock hitting the ground added to the hovering anxiety. The gates screamed in a language not meant for mortal ears followed by a hiss.

A large black cat arched its back, fur standing on end, one paw taking a swipe at Noah before waddling through to the road.

"Mrs. Furry-paws!" Vic screamed, rushing to his precious pet.

Noah tried to hide a snicker. Losing the battle, a snort escaped, followed by a hearty laugh. "I'm sorry," he said, gaining his composure.

Vic struggled picking up his cat. The ratio of man to pet wasn't in his favour. It didn't help that he was smaller sized to begin with, his weight and height well under national averages.

Add on top the sheer massiveness of Mrs. Furry-paws and Noah wasn't the only one trying to hold back a few chuckles.

"Did you miss me?" Vic cooed, kissing black fur. "You must be hungry. We'll get you straight home for something to eat."

The situation proved too much for Noah. Unable to control his emotions, he burst out into a second round of laughter.

"Is something funny?" Vic asked.

"It's just," Noah said, still laughing. He held up a finger, trying to gain enough composure to finish his sentence. "It's just... that cat wasn't going to starve." The hysterics continued. Vic was an enabler.

"Don't you body shame Mrs. Furry-paws," Vic ordered in a stern voice. He reaffirmed his grip on his pet, puckering his lips. "Don't you listen to that bad man. You are perfect just the way you are." He rubbed his nose in her fur. "I think we'll go home now, if you don't mind."

"I'll lead the way," Bessie offered, tapping her flashlight a few times before switching it on. "We'll get Mrs. Furry-paws some dinner and treats."

"Perhaps we all should say good night," Jewel suggested. "I think the strain of the evening might have been too much for all of us."

Al motioned to the other officers to lead the rest of the group to their respective homes. He watched them as they each reached their front porches and glanced back. The street lights hummed, warming up to brighten the road, but that wasn't what caught their attention. The upper window of Eight, Nine Street had gone dark.

"Imagine that," Al said, shaking his head. "Some odd coincidences have been happening in these parts. I guess we won't be needing that generator of yours after all. Can I give you..."

Al turned around. He glanced from side to side. Mr. Body was gone, leaving him scratching his head. Lips pursed together, his hand held the locked heavy padlock dangling from chains on the closed gates. "How?" He spun around looking for an explanation to his own question, but found nothing.

"Everything okay, boss?" Bessie asked, returning.

"I lost a body," Al joked. "I think we might win an award for most bizarre case for this one."

"Roger that," Bessie replied, chuckling. "If you don't mind, I think I've had enough of Nine Street for one night."

9 Nine Street

Noah pushed his hands into his pant pockets. He glanced from side to side at empty stone pedestals before climbing the steps. There wasn't any need to even slow his pace at the top. The front door creaked open, acknowledging his arrival.

He headed straight to the parlour, the scent of burning wood his guide. From outside the double doors he watched the shadows of flickering flames dancing as if attending their own formal ball. He stopped for a moment, savouring the crackling noise of wood turning to ash - the ultimate symbol of total destruction.

From where he stood, he could see the bare crossed legs of a woman - her feet adorned with high heels, one dangling half-off.

"You disappeared rather quickly tonight," Noah stated.

"No one noticed," the woman replied.

"They could have," Noah argued.

"But they didn't. I am not yet strong enough to pass through gates or simply will doors to open. You know that. I need time to get used to this body. If I had stayed, I wouldn't be here right now."

"I suppose that's true," Noah said. "But too many things went wrong with our plans and that leaves us in a situation. Tell me, what made you take control of the wrong body?"

"It was necessary," the woman snapped. "How was I to know Fellannie had a protective talisman? It was too strong for me in my weakened condition. An opportunity showed itself and I took it."

"These people are quite surprising - so resilient," Noah stated. "So tell me, how are you liking Claire's body?"

"It's younger and more attractive than the other one. I think I like it, don't you?" Claire replied. "Your idea was brilliant. I never would have known that a gas leak could create the same symptoms as a demonic possession."

"I wouldn't have either if it weren't for Noah Body's knowledge of all things strange," he explained. "It was a sheer luck he showed up here interested in the past. It made him such an easy target. He practically gave me his life. Of course, I took advantage of the offer."

"What about the others?" Claire asked. "When can we aid in their release? Soon, I hope."

"We can't risk it," Noah said, his face stern. "If anyone suspects, they will drag another set of witches in here and send us back to hell. We lost control of the plan. We should have taken more of the houses than we ended up with. You should be happy you have your sister to visit with. That reminds me, thank her for making that appearance in the window. It smoothed things over with the outsiders." His gaze locked on the contents of the fireplace, flames blazing to new heights.

"Don't be so hard on yourself. You couldn't have known things would go the way they did," Claire said, rubbing his shoulders. "Eve should have been carted off to jail for attempted murder and her house left empty. I still can't believe how that little vixen lied. Imagine being able to convince everyone the hypnosis didn't work."

"Yes, a woman after my own heart," Noah stated. "If she didn't have feelings for the police officer, that black soul of hers might have made for a good Allie."

"Your heart belongs to me!" Claire exclaimed. "We are bound to each other for eternity. Don't forget that."

"I haven't, my love," Noah offered. "Nonetheless, it will be more difficult to take her home away from her now. You also need to keep your pets under control. One of them was seen. That could have been another costly mistake."

The woman cackled. "I can't help it if you locked a cat in here with them. You know gargoyles hate cats. It threw him off his game, the poor dear. At least he managed to get the job done."

"Yes, that is something," Noah admitted. "Although I had hoped for an untimely end to Mr. And Mrs. Rhe." He made his way to a tray of alcohol. "Drink?"

"I have one, thanks," the woman said.

"We will have to hold off for a bit now," Noah said. "Let things cool down before going ahead with our plans."

"Why?"

"You know why!" Noah yelled. "They came too close to figuring it all out. We can't afford to make any more mistakes." He chugged back his drink before turning to face her. "We have control of four houses. That's less than half. Once we have the majority, our strength will grow. Then, and only then, will we be ready for anything this world tries to throw at us."

Claire howled a laugh. "How long?"

"As long as it takes," Noah replied. "We were trapped for centuries, I think we can wait a decade or two to take over the world." He raised his glass. "To the end of all things good."

Claire returned the motion with her own glass. "To the end of all things good." She took a sip. "I suppose a few decades isn't too long to wait, as long as I have you to play with."

"That you do," Noah said, a grin creeping over his face. He pulled Claire close, their lips meeting in passion. "I'm glad you have a body again. It'll make passing the time go so much faster." He swept her off her feet, the two disappearing up the stairs.

Message from the Author

I hope you enjoyed *Twisted Tales of a Dead End Street*. This has been one of my favourite stories to work on and I wanted to share with you how this book came into being. You see, I belong to a writer's group.

The Brantford Writer's Circle meets once a month. I was invited to join shortly after I moved to the Bell City. Accepting that offer was one of the best decisions I have ever made. I can't stress enough how much inspiration you can find with the investment of only a few hours.

Different people take turns leading the meetings, each setting the activities for their evening. It could be anything from poetry readings to guest speakers and sometimes a fun game or two. There is also usually a writing prompt in which those participating have a set amount of time to write a story based on a particular list of ideas. At the end, the stories created are read out loud.

I am flawed; damaged goods so to speak. There really isn't any other way to say it. I have spent the better part of my years of writing going through multiple drafts and using beta readers. That is all before it goes to my editor and through proof reading. I cringe at the thought of forcing anyone to hear the initial scribblings I call a first draft. That's why I don't, even at the meetings.

One particular night, fellow author, Rosie Burthom, planned a page full of the most unusual writing prompts I'd ever seen. I sat and wrote up an outline for several stories based on them, but as always, it was nothing worth reading. I did, however, promise I'd work on it further at home. In the end, I did a little more than I had initially planned.

This book includes my interpretation of quite a few of the prompts that were listed that day, each one hidden in the chapters - an Easter egg hunt of sorts. How much fun would finding them all be for a meeting?

There are writer's clubs in almost every town or city. Joining one could be a step towards writing something amazing. So what are you waiting for?

Remember:

Anything and everything could be the plot for your next story. Imagination is all you need to tie it all together.

Happy reading & writing...

C.A. King

Other Titles from C.A. King

The Portal Prophecies

These great titles in C.A. King's The Portal Prophecies series are available now at most online book retailers:

A Keeper's Destiny

A Halloween's Curse

Frost Bitten

Sleeping Sands

Deadly Perceptions

Finding Balance

The prophecies are the key to their survival. Can they solve them in time?

Shattering the Effects of Time

Join the Shinning brothers, Jessie, Dezi and Pete as they set out on a quest to save their younger sister. No magic known to them or their friends has ever been able to reverse the grip of time. A few legends, however, exist mentioning ancient items that may hold the key to do exactly that.

This brand new series will take you on a search for the Fountain of Youth and Mermaids; a quest for the Holy Grail; a trip to visit Daryl the mountain guru, in the hunt for the Cinamani Stone; on a search for Ambrosia, the food of the Gods; and other adventures.

Surviving the Sins: Answering the Call

The prophecies are being rewritten. This time someone is using the seven deadly sins: Lust; Gluttony; Greed; Sloth; Wrath; Envy; and Pride, to unlock an ancient evil. The book falls into Jade's hands to answer destiny's call. Can she survive the sins?

Surviving the Sins: Pride

No one is safe when a witch's pride is at stake.

Prudance is back in Pewterclaw, and she isn't about to give up her prestigious status without a fight - especially not because of vampires. As an eighth-generation witch, she plans to do whatever it takes to stop the proposed new legislation from becoming law, including waking the dead for help.

Humility isn't in her vocabulary. With an ego spinning out of control and ancestral power at her fingertips, Prudance weaves a plot to keep Jade and Gavin separated. Will it be enough to satisfy the spirits she summoned?

When her pride costs more than she bargained for, someone has to pay the tab - but who will it be?

Surviving the Sins: Lust

What Mother doesn't know won't hurt her.

Lucinda has spent her entire existence running The Organization and looking after Mother's needs without complaint. That's about to change. A burning desire had manifested inside her - one she could no longer deny... Lust.

When Constable Safron Black shows up unexpected with news of an imprisoned God, Lucinda unravels. With power fuelling her passion, she'll do anything to make Morynx her mate.

****

Jade and her friends find themselves at a standstill. They have already failed to stop Pride from completing its task and they haven't located any victims for the other six sins. A strange fire in the municipal office puts them hot on the trail of what could be answers. Will they be in time to stop the dial from moving and further opening the way for Morynx?

When Leaves Fall: A Different Point of View Story

Ralph wakes up to what others only experience in a nightmare. Chained to a shed, he has no idea where he is, or who his captor is. His memories a blurred at best. As the days press on he finds himself experiencing a roller coaster of feelings. Hunger, thirst and pain become his only companions. Flashbacks of a happier time are all he has to keep him going. As his situation deteriorates, he finds himself doubting the very things he wants most - a family.

When Leaves Fall is a dramatic-thriller with a twist. Keep the tissue box close for the ending.

Tomoiya's Story

A Vampire Tale. She had a secret but she wasn't the only one who had something to hide.

Book I ~ *Escape to Darkness*

Book II ~ *Collection Tears*

Book III~ *Coming Soon*

Peach Coloured Daisies: A Cursed by the Gods Story

He couldn't die. An ancient curse meant she always did. This time, that was going to change - one way or another.

When Daisy's grandmother, her last living relative, passes away, she doesn't know where to turn. Things go from bad to worse when a local psychic tells her about a curse. Alone and confused, she ends up in front of her college professor's office, ready to cry her heart out in his arms.

Matt Demi might be the son of a God, but he's living the life of a cursed man. He's had to watch the woman he loves die on her twenty-first birthday countless times. Nothing he does seems to be able to affect the outcome. When she shows up at his office scared out of her wits by a psychic's prediction, he vows this time will be different.

With only three days, Matt will need to embrace a side of him he swore off long ago to save her, but will he lose himself in the process?

Flower Shields: A Four Horsemen Novel

Meet the four horsemen: Michael, Gabrielle, Uriel and Raphael. For centuries their job has been to guard the gates of hell, making sure they never open. Without the keys, there was never any real threat. That's about to change. There are rumours on the horizon that demon followers unearthed scrolls that explain exactly how to find the lost keys. This new battle is a race to see which side locates them first.

Michael couldn't care less about the love story behind how and why the world was created. In fact, nothing matters to him other than keeping the gates to hell closed. If one of the lost keys ever fell into the wrong hands, all humanity would be doomed. He's not going to let that happen - at any cost.

****

Tara's life is nothing short of a disaster. She's managed to flunk out of college with about the same amount of dignity as every relationship she's been in. The only constant in her life has been her love for flowers. When she's attacked at work, a stranger comes to her aid. Michael might be good-looking, but he's also arrogant, bossy and crazy. He's also her only chance to figure out who attacked her and why. Should she follow her heart and trust him - or listen to her head and run?

Miracles Not Included

A heartfelt romantic story about: life; love; loss; and learning to love again. If only life came with instructions and a warning label ~ Miracles Not Included.

****

Chris was born to be a writer. Even the smallest of details couldn't pass without notice, often becoming part of a plot for her next novel. The one thing she never saw coming was her husband's sudden illness.

Jason loved his wife from the moment they met. Nothing could ever change that - nothing except the death sentence he'd been handed - a terminal cancer diagnosis.

His story was ending: Hers was starting a new chapter and more than one miracle was needed to turn the page.